Rhythm & Muse

Rhythm & muse

INDIA HILL BROWN

Quill Tree Books
An Imprint of HarperCollinsPublishers

Quill Tree Books is an imprint of HarperCollins Publishers.

Rhythm & Muse
Copyright © 2023 by India Hill Brown
All rights reserved. Printed in the United States of America.
No part of this book may be used or reproduced in any manner whatsoever
without written permission except in the case of brief quotations embodied in
critical articles and reviews. For information, address HarperCollins Publishers,
195 Broadway, New York, NY 10007.
www.epicreads.com
Library of Congress Control Number: 2023930010
ISBN 978-0-06-321755-3
Typography by David Curtis
23 24 25 26 27 LBC 5 4 3 2 1
First Edition

To Bear and August, my Rhythms
To Rob, my Muse

For Eli, my little brother

For Donovan, my little brother-in-law

Rhythm & Muse

01: Intro

I look into her dark brown eyes and grab her hand. I hear the crowd faintly cheering our names in a beautiful song as I spin her around and around, the sound of her laughter drowning out the bass of the music playing.

"Delia! Darren!" the crowd continues.

"Delia! Darren!"

I pull her closer.

"Delia!"

"DARREN!"

The deep voice of my best friend, Justin, interrupts my daydream and fills my ears. Delia and the crowd melt away around me, replaced with the parking lot of the corner store.

"Did you hear me?" he says, waving his ashy hand in front of my face. He scoffs. "Don't tell me you were having another Delia Daydream?"

"I wasn't," I say uncomfortably, defensively. "I heard you."

"Then what did I say?"

I pause. I have no idea. "Hopefully, you asked to borrow some lotion."

Justin sucks his teeth as he gets out of the car. It's lunchtime, and we're off campus. We just grabbed lunch and we're at the corner store grabbing some snacks to get us through the rest of the day.

"Darren, come on, this is serious. We're *juniors* now," Justin says as we walk in and spot our go-to snacks right in the first aisle. He grabs his, barbecue chips and lemonade, and I grab mine, spicy chips and a bottle of water, and we quickly pay for them and head back out.

"What's serious?" I ask noncommittally as we crunch through the gravel toward Justin's car. The remote on his key chain beeps as we approach. He presses the button to start the car.

"*This.* I've been having to pull you out of these Delia Daydreams for too long now, and they got worse over the summer. I've had enough; *you've* had enough. Either ask Delia out or move on."

I almost stop in my tracks, but I keep walking so he won't know what he's saying is actually ringing true today.

"I get it," he continues. "Last year, she had a boyfriend already. You didn't want to be disrespectful. This year, though? Just walk up to her, talk to her, and ask her out! She'll only say yes or no."

But that's the thing, I think to myself. She *can* say no, and if she does, it'll be over. No more what ifs, no more Delia Daydreams. I'd eventually move on, and that would be that. The thought was kind of sad.

But all I say is "You make it sound so simple."

And it's really not. Delia Dawson, known affectionately as Dillie, creator of the newish, hit podcast *Dillie D in the Place to Be*, transferred to Jamison High School during the second semester of our sophomore year. When I saw her walking the halls for the first time, I immediately knew she was The One. Well, if she wants to be.

Her presence commands attention: her skin is a warm, rich brown that looks like it glows from the inside out; her lips are full and pink and always shiny with lip gloss, spread apart in a genuine smile or a sneer when someone around her says something ridiculous—the kind of sneer that makes me feel glad I'm not on the receiving end of it.

When she first arrived at Jamison, I joined the chorus of the other kids around school who wanted to know, "Who is *she*?" *Dillie D in the Place to Be* hadn't taken off yet, so no one knew much about her. From what I heard, she had a boyfriend from her old school, but they broke up a little while after she transferred, and it ended kind of badly. She started the podcast shortly after that because she wanted an outlet to vent her feelings.

He broke up with her on Valentine's Day. *Valentine's Day.*

I knew better than to try to ask her on a date during February, March, or even April, but a lot of guys didn't. She took her thoughts to the podcast, discussing some of the worst pickup lines she'd received, and even though she kept their names anonymous, those guys knew they'd struck out. When I do finally get the courage to ask Delia out, everything *has* to be perfect. I can't help but feel like I'm only going to get one chance to do it right.

It's not like we don't casually talk. We've had a few classes together, and even attend the same church. We'll speak sometimes during Morning Fellowship, in the hallway, or at football games when we see each other. But that's enough for now. I don't want to say too much until she knows I'm interested in her—then she can see me as a potential boyfriend and not just some random guy she sees around.

"*Darren*," Justin says again, angrily.

"I'm sorry, man. What?"

Justin sighs, rubbing his hand over his head as if me and my Delia Daydreams are the most taxing thing in his life right now. Maybe we are. Justin pretty much has it all. He's always the life of the party, liked by everyone; he has a huge house, a nice car, and is back "on" with his on-again, off-again girlfriend, Tiffany.

"Look, just ask her out," he says again. He has a way of homing in on an issue and not letting it go until it's resolved. I prefer to let my thoughts settle before speaking, but that's how we're different.

"I know it's not that simple, but this relationship you have going on with Delia inside your head is creepy. Imagine what she'd think about it?"

I consider this. It seems like everything is a lot safer inside my head. But the last thing I want is for Delia to see me as creepy.

We *are* juniors now. Upperclassmen. This is serious business. I even have a meeting with my guidance counselor after lunch to talk more about the next two years. Maybe daydreaming about my crush is underclassman behavior. It was the first week of school, time for a fresh start.

"Aiight," I tell Justin as he pulls out of the trash-filled parking lot of the corner store and back to school, the smell of our chicken sandwiches filling up the car. The radio turns on automatically. It takes a second to figure out what the song is since the bass in Justin's car stereo overpowers the lyrics. The seats and windows vibrate in that way we all know and love, every time the beat drops. When the verse starts, I realize it's that new singer, Louis Dot Williams, who a lot of people like but who, quite frankly, struggles with his notes live.

"Man!" Justin slaps his steering wheel. "Whew! This man is a lyrical *genius*! Do you hear that?"

"No," I say. Between the bass and the auto-tune, how can I?

Justin shakes his head. "You don't get it. Louis Dot is talking about some real stuff. It sounds just *like* what me and Tiffany are going through."

I say nothing, because this is Justin's favorite artist and we've gotten into it countless times before about our differences of opinion. I like clear, difficult notes, key changes, and bridges, and this song doesn't have any of that. In the words of the late, great Whitney Houston, "I listen to *singers*." I open my bag and pull out a handful of curly fries, ignoring Justin's warning about not getting crumbs everywhere because he just got his car cleaned.

My mind drifts back to what Justin said about Dillie. "How should I do it, then?"

I genuinely don't know. I know Justin will, though, because when he and Tiffany are Off Again, Justin wastes no time going out on dates with other girls, at Jamison and beyond. Tiffany does the same thing, dating other guys. It's weird; they'll casually date other people, but everyone, including the two of them, knows they'll eventually get back together, and the new "daters" know to tread lightly, never catching serious feelings. Ask either Tiffany or Justin, and they'd both tell you in a heartbeat that they are getting married one day, and that this chaotic system just works for them right now.

I don't want Delia and me to have to have that sort of system. Never mind. Maybe I shouldn't have asked Justin for his advice after all.

I'm starting to think that maybe he forgot about my question since his favorite singer is on the radio, but this is his thing: helping, giving solicited and unsolicited advice. So he takes the bait before I can take it back.

"You could always do the obvious thing: walk up to her and ask her," he answers, as he turns onto the street our school is on.

This is true, but not as simple as it sounds. I've seen dudes crash and burn in front of Delia, whether it's because she's with her friends and they did the dirty work for her, or she waved them off herself, thanking them for trying. Even when I do try to talk to her about any old thing, there's rarely any time for that. She's always hustling to her next class, the library, to work on her podcast, always on the brink of being late. The thought of me stammering through asking her out and making her even later to her next commitment makes me queasy.

"That's an option," I say, carefully wiping the crumbs I've spilled on the seat into a napkin before Justin notices.

"You could also shoot your shot digitally. You know, Clip Message her."

Hm. Messaging her on social media. I was better with words written than words said. Maybe I could do that.

"Another option" is all I say.

As we pull into the parking lot of Jamison High, I'm thinking about the places I can ask Delia out on a date. Maybe we could go to a local concert together, or grab a bite to eat. Or both.

Justin and I grab our lunches and snacks and walk to the main courtyard, where mostly everyone else is walking around, talking, eating. We head toward our usual spot, the brick wall, which is low enough to hop on and get a good view of everything that's going on around us.

I notice her walking past the brick wall, straight toward us, with two of her friends.

Delia.

Justin eyes me pointedly, then veers off to the right, leaving me to walk toward her and her group of friends alone. He must think I'm going to ask her right now. *Now*, as if I'd say something unrehearsed. As if I'd had a chance to think about what to say, or to consider every scenario in which she could say no.

Or yes.

But I have to say something because she's right in front of me.

"What's up, Delia? Mia, Julie," I say, pretending that I'm seeing her for the first time.

Mia and Julie wave at me and keep walking. Delia slows down, just a step.

"Hey, Darren." She eyes me up and down. "I like that shirt."

The navy-blue button-up shirt that I almost didn't buy because it seemed like a beast to iron, the shirt that I almost didn't iron *today* because I was running late, but I decided to anyway?

I've never been so thankful for my iron.

"Thank you," I say, and for just another second or two, she's still standing there. Should I compliment her back? Should I say something about the iron?

Or maybe, just maybe, I could just ask her out.

"*Dillie!* Come on, I'm hungry!" Mia says, waving her over, a small frown on her face. I sympathize. My stomach is growling, too. Those curly fries didn't fill me up at all.

But—

"I'm coming!" Dillie says, walking away from me. I register the curve of her hips as she walks away, but keep my eyes up, in case she turns around.

She does.

"What were you saying, Darren?" she asks, walking backward now.

"Oh, uh—I was saying I like your shirt, too."

She smiles, a brilliant white smile that could disarm anyone.

"Thanks," she says, and turns around and jogs toward her friends.

I'm grinning, walking to where Justin is sitting, thinking of how our interaction is enough to fuel my daydreams for the entire week.

Justin is frowning at me, though, the same one that Mia had, but he's still working on his lunch, so it can't be from hunger.

"What?" I ask.

"What happened?"

"It wasn't the right time." And it really wasn't. It didn't feel right.

Justin groans.

"You saw her, she was in a hurry, as usual."

Justin finishes off the rest of his chicken sandwich and balls up the foil it was wrapped in. He shoots it toward the trash can; it spins around the rim and pops back out. He groans again, hops off the wall, walks toward it, and picks it up.

"Darren, look. *You* are this piece of foil," he says, holding it up to me.

I raise an eyebrow.

"You were shooting your shot, everything was prepped for success, but you jumped back and chickened out."

"That's what just happened? Or are your shooting skills just off?"

"No. Listen. I'm doing this because we're basically brothers and I'm trying to help you. You gotta get out of your own head, man. Ask her out or leave her alone."

As much as I hate to admit it, Justin and his unsolicited chicken sandwich analogy are right. This is the year that I ask Delia out. If she's uninterested, I could live with that. But at least I'd have gathered up the courage to ask. At least I'd know.

I take the wrapper from Justin and toss it toward the trash can and it lands perfectly. He scoffs, and I shrug.

If only dating were that easy.

02: Brainstorm

I walk into the career development office, still buzzing from the compliment Dillie gave me and my non-wrinkled, navy-blue shirt, and have a seat.

After a few minutes, my guidance counselor, Mrs. Thompson, peeks her head out from around the corner where her office is. "Darren! Hello! Please, come on in!"

I get up from where I was sitting in the lobby, pulled out of the trance caused by the receptionist clicking away on her laptop and the trickling sound from the water coming out of the little fountain they've placed on the coffee table in front of me.

"How are you?" Mrs. Thompson says this so enthusiastically that for a second, I wonder if she's going to reach out for a hug. She doesn't.

She's cool, though. A far cry from my old guidance counselor, Mrs. Earnhardt. If you were making anything less than a B in any class, she'd tell you with the straightest face that college didn't look like it was the best option for you, and maybe you should try being a mechanic.

Don't get me wrong, being a mechanic is great and all, but still. She wasn't exactly the most encouraging when it came to going to college and seemed weirdly obsessed with suggesting this one specific alternate career.

I don't know if she left on her own accord or if she just got too many complaints from crying juniors who knew nothing about fixing cars, but she's gone now. I like Mrs. Thompson, though, because she actually gets to know us enough to make suggestions that fit with our personalities, and she's super nice, so she's the exact opposite of Mrs. Earnhardt. And since she's new, I don't have to hear about being the Great Zoe Armstrong's little brother every time I enter her office.

"Have a seat." She gestures to the armchair in front of her desk. I sink into it. Even her chairs are nicer than Mrs. Earnhardt's were.

"How is junior year treating you so far?" she asks, typing something into her computer and glancing over at me.

I look at the poster behind her, which says, "Your Only Limit Is Your Mind!" in bold, blue lettering.

"Um. So far so good. You know, for the first few days."

"Junior year flies by," she says, clicking some more buttons with her mouse. I assume she's pulling up my file. "The next thing you know, you'll be committing to a college and trying on your cap and gown."

"That's what I hear," I say. My sister just told me the same thing.

"Your grades are still stellar," she says. "Community service, excellent. Hmm."

Her brow furrows for a second, and I wonder why. I haven't even so much as gotten a detention before.

"Extracurricular activities?" she asks.

"Oh, I do a lot for my church," I say. "Vacation Bible school, morning guest greeter, you name it."

"I see," she says. "It seems like you used to—you were in both church choir *and* school chorus up until first semester last year. What happened?"

I just stare at her. Mrs. Earnhardt would've never asked this. Or noticed it, in the way that Mrs. Thompson does. "What *happened*?" she asks again. She shakes her head, as if my extracurricular activities, or lack thereof, are really stressing her out.

"Nothing happened," I say. "It was just a hobby, anyway. I just got too busy for it. Studying and stuff. You know."

Mrs. Thompson looks at me squarely. She does not believe me.

"I mean, you know, chorus and choir travel a lot," I continue on.

She says nothing.

I clear my throat and try again. "My voice started changing around that time so I didn't know if I was a tenor or a baritone."

I mean, it's not *totally* a lie. My voice was changing at that time and combined with nerves and other things, those were just some of the reasons that my last performance was such a bust.

I shake my head. I don't want to think about that right now.

"Darren," Mrs. Thompson says. "Tell me. What do you do for fun?"

"I do a lot of things for fun," I say, and the lie just falls out my mouth and clunks onto the table.

"Tell me," she pries.

"I—listen to music. I do love to listen to music. Hang out with friends. Grab a bite to eat."

There's a singing-sized hole in the middle of the room and Mrs. Thompson sees it.

"Look, forget this college talk for a second," she says, and I raise my eyebrow because is that something a guidance counselor is supposed to say?

She clicks around on her computer some more and looks back at me. "We've already talked about your top three schools, and we know you're very likely to be accepted into all of them. You have the grades, the community service, the SAT scores." She lowers her voice. "This is your junior year. It seems to me you quit something you love and you should do what you love *now*. Have some fun while you don't have to worry about paying rent or washing your own clothes."

"I wash my own clothes now," I point out.

She ignores me. "I'll let you in on a secret. I did some digging and I asked the chorus director about you. He says he has no idea why you quit, and that you have such a bright future ahead of you as a singer. I can even hear it in your talking voice! You're

on the right track. It's okay if you—you know, shake it up a bit."
She does a little shoulder move.

I look around for a brief second and wonder if I'm getting
pranked.

"Um. Okay. Thanks, Mrs. Thompson." I put both my hands
on either side of my armchair, preparing to get up. She looks at
me and nods as a sign of dismissal. Thankfully.

"Well. I'll see you in a few weeks," I say. What a strange meeting. I did not come here to get grilled on why I quit singing. It's
not her business, is it? I can feel the moment everything changed
trying to creep back to my mind and I shake my head to get it
out. Mid-headshake, I catch a picture of a woman with blond,
extremely curly hair and extremely red lipstick on the table
beside the door. She's wearing a sparkly black dress and holding
a microphone. It's an old picture and it's autographed.

"Is this you, Mrs. Thompson?" I can't help but ask.

"Darren, listen to me. Think about what I said!"

03: "Turn it on!"

"Son!"

My dad has the uncanny ability to know exactly when I'm about to walk into any room he's in. Justin and I are walking up the steps to the front porch of my house. I pull out my key and insert it into the lock.

"Son!" he yells again, just as I twist the key and push the door open. I find him in the living room, hovering over the coffee table, his brow furrowed in concentration as he stares at something on top of it.

"Um—yes?" I glance at Justin. He shrugs. There was always something random going on at my house.

"Darren, I can't get this dang thing to turn on. I think it's broken. I do not feel like having to go back out today and get this fixed!"

"It's probably not broken," I say, walking over to the rectangular speaker. "When you want it to play music or something, you have to say, 'Turn it on.'" Instantly, the entire speaker lights up.

"Oh, wow! That's amazing! It's amazing what they're

doing in technology these days, isn't it, Dorothea?" he yells to my mother, who's coming down the stairs.

That's the thing about my parents. They're always yelling. Not arguing. *Yelling.* Dad uses the same volume with us no matter what. It doesn't matter if we're in the same room, if I'm upstairs and he's downstairs, if we're at the library or at a basketball game. Maybe that's why I'm a man of not-so-many words. I'm always getting drowned out by my dad. And Mom. And best friend. And sister, when she's here.

"It sure is, honey," my mom says as she walks over and gives me a kiss on the cheek. "Hey, Darren. Hey, Justin. How was school?" She moves past us to my dad where they share a long embrace, as if they hadn't seen each other no longer ago than ten minutes before we got here.

If there was a poster couple for the most sickeningly lovey-dovey, it would be my parents. They dated in high school, then college, and married soon after. And they're always doing something together—ballroom dancing, movie dates, trying and failing to figure out the latest in technology. It's a little embarrassing, especially in public, but I can't pretend that it doesn't make me smile a little. Maybe that's why I have my heart set on one girl and one girl only. Maybe I just want what they have. Only . . . not as loud.

I shrug. "It was cool." I eye Justin to let him know not to say anything about Dillie, but he's not meeting my stare, which isn't a good sign.

"You met with your guidance counselor today, right? How did that go?"

I feel like I mentioned this appointment offhandedly, once, at the beginning of the week, but leave it to my mom to remember.

"It was cool," I repeat. "Everything is looking the way it's supposed to. Grades are good. Of course, I have community service. She said I just need, um . . ." I remember Mrs. Thompson's strange comments asking about my extracurricular activities and what I do for fun.

I *do* have fun. I love basketball, getting food, going to the movies. I just prefer not to hear the criticism of others about things personal to me, like singing, when I can help it. I consider my life a play—better yet, one of those one-person plays. I'm writing the script and rehearsing it, and rarely do I like to do improv. And *never* will I read the reviews.

"You're doing it again," Justin says in a singsongy way, nudging me. I look up to see my mom looking at me curiously while my dad leaves to check on whatever is cooking in the kitchen.

"Doing what?" My mom has these round, wide eyes and this way about her that makes you feel like she genuinely cares about what you're saying or going through. She pulls it right out of you. "What do you need?"

"She said I needed—"

"Mrs. Armstrong, maybe you can help us," Justin interrupts, throwing his arm over my shoulder.

My head whips toward his in a silent question. *What are you doing?*

Justin shrugs unapologetically. As if he were doing this for my own good.

"Mrs. Armstrong, our Darren here is lovesick. He's been crushing on the same girl for over a year, and I fear that this crush in his head is taking over his life. I expressed my concerns today by telling him he should simply ask the woman of his heart out, so he can have an answer and move on with his life."

Is he serious? I can't *wait* to pay Justin back for this.

My mom puts her hands over her heart and sighs. "Oh, Darren, that's beautiful. Is it Delia or is it someone else?"

I sputter. "Mama—what?"

She looks at me, her eyes twinkling. "Darren, I was born *at* night, not *last* night. Anyone could see you have a crush on her."

Is that true? Not the part about her being born at night, but can everyone tell I have a crush on Dillie? Including . . . her?

"Um—" I start.

My mom continues. "Oh, I know her mom, you know her family goes to the same church as us. Oh, I could just *imagine* the prom pictures—"

"Whoa, Mama." I hold up my hand. "I haven't even asked her out yet."

"Asked who out?" I hear my dad ask as he walks around the corner and out of the kitchen, holding what looks like a dish of lasagna in his hands. He sets it on the dining room table, which is in an open area off the living room. "And dinner's ready. Justin, you're more than welcome to stay."

I sigh as Justin grins and says thank you. Just like that, the conversation continues to revolve around my nonexistent love life. This is going to turn into one of those things where everyone weighs in on my life, since they think I don't care, when I actually *do*. I just . . . prefer to take my time, make sure everything is right before I do anything rash.

"Delia Dawson. Renée and Patrick Dawson's daughter," my mom says as we make our way to the dining room table. We pause briefly, bowing our heads and closing our eyes as she says grace over our food. My mom picks the conversation back up seamlessly. "She's a beautiful girl, bright head on her shoulders."

"Oh, yeah, I know who you're talking about," Dad says, cutting into the lasagna. "She does the church announcements sometimes, doesn't she?"

"Yes," I say, but my answer is drowned out by Mom's.

"Well, now, son, if you needed help asking her out, you could've just asked me. This is my area of expertise."

"Now, I wouldn't say *that*, Wyatt," my mom says. "You pretty much just fell into my lap. Literally. And started talking to me. And *that* was over twenty years ago."

I try to picture myself accidentally falling on Delia's lap and all I can think of is her shoving me off in confusion.

"I *am* an expert! It worked, didn't it?"

Mom rolls her eyes playfully and Dad smiles in return.

"Maybe you should just tell her how you feel. It can't hurt, can it?" Mom says.

"That's what I said, Mrs. Armstrong." Justin helps himself to a piece of lasagna. "We were also thinking maybe . . . maybe he can message her on eClips."

"Oh, come on, social media!" Dad throws his hands up in the air dramatically. "She goes to school with you, doesn't she? I'm sure she would appreciate you confidently walking up to her and asking."

The table is quiet, and I realize that everyone is actually waiting on me to speak.

"It's a thought," I say, taking a bite of the lasagna, then following up with a gulp of sweet tea.

"Son, let me tell you." Dad points his fork at me. "It's all about the charm. Like, Prince Charming."

"Now, I wouldn't say that, either. Charm can be deceiving," Mom says, referencing her favorite Bible scripture.

"Well, yeah, but Darren is actually charming, so it's okay. Right?" Dad chews a piece of lasagna and swallows it. "You just have to know how to turn it on."

"Turned on: please respond with your music selection." The little speaker on the coffee table beeps.

Dad's eyes light up. "Hey! It worked!"

04: Collab

After a dinner featuring everyone's opinions on what I should say to Dillie, Justin heads up to my room to grab the basketball he'd left behind a couple of days ago. He's on the way back downstairs when he gets a text message.

"Hey, Jerrod wants us to come to the studio with him tonight to preview this new song of his."

Jerrod is Justin's cousin, a nice enough guy who goes to another high school across town. He has rap dreams but can't really rap. I think he knows it deep down, but you can't blame the guy for trying.

"Cool. Just let me grab my jacket," I say, passing Justin on the stairs to my room. It was Friday night, and I didn't have any plans.

I walk back downstairs to find my mom and dad dancing with each other to one of "their songs" as it finishes.

"We're headed out. I'm not staying out too late," I call to my parents.

They look over from their embrace and smile at me. "Okay, y'all be safe!" my mom says.

"I guess this ol' technology isn't terrible, is it, son?" my dad asks as the song ends. "Forever My Lady" by Jodeci. It blares from the speaker. "Y'all don't know nothin' about this! This is old school!" Dad yells.

"Dad. You say this *every time* you play this song, and you play it at least three times a week. I know it word-for-word by now."

He spins my mom around and sings a few lyrics, off-key. "Son, if you're feeling stumped, I'll say this. Sometimes you can let music do the talking." He dips my mom backward and she giggles.

"Noted, Dad," I say, chuckling a little at them. "Y'all have fun."

We instinctively walk to Justin's car instead of mine since it's newer and nicer, leaving the muffled harmonies, my dad's howling, and my mom's laughing behind us. We drive to the studio, the rap songs on Justin's playlist wrapping around my thoughts. Pretty soon, we're on a modest street with a shopping center, walking to the door that says Incredible Beatz on a neon sign above it. The *E* in Beatz isn't lit up.

We're greeted by the sound of rapping that has long since left the beat playing over it. We walk into one of the two studio rooms, and I'm ready to set my poker face on. Jerrod is *really* terrible at this.

There's an engineer there, also poker-faced, which is probably with much practice, as he owns the place and sees a lot of talent and lack thereof come through. Jerrod sees us and rushes from the booth to the other side of the glass.

"What's up, y'all, what's up," he says quickly, dapping us up—he even talks in an odd cadence. Jerrod is a slimmer version of Justin, a tall, dark-skinned guy, and is always wearing opaque sunglasses and his beloved platinum grill over his bottom teeth. He takes off the shades he was wearing.

"Nothing, man, we just came from Darren's and—wow, you look terrible."

Justin may have been brash, but he wasn't lying. Jerrod's eyes are red and he has bags under them.

Jerrod heaves a long sigh. "Man, Destiny and I broke up."

My eyebrows lift. "Really?"

"What happened?" Justin asks.

I didn't know Destiny very well, but Jerrod talked about her whenever we saw him.

"Just a big argument. She doesn't support my dreams."

"Of . . . being a rapper?" Justin and I glance at each other.

"Yeah," Jerrod says. "And that's important to any relationship, right? Support?"

"Uhh . . ." I don't know what to say. Jerrod is just plain not good at this, and maybe Destiny told him so.

"*Exactly*. Exactly." Jerrod nods, as if we agree with him. "I'm writing a song about it. I only laid the first verse down. Y'all wanna hear it?"

We both nod and take seats in two chairs beside the engineer. He presses play.

The track is nice. Smooth with hard-hitting beats and piano notes. The lyrics are okay, as he pretty much raps about what he just told us: reaching for his dreams even when those around him don't support them. How his heart is broken.

But the delivery is just not there, and that's what makes the difference.

Maybe it's something he could learn, I wonder, since I know he's going to ask us how we feel once it's done playing. Maybe he could tailor beats to his off-beat delivery. Maybe it could be his trademark.

The verse stops and the track plays a little longer without words until the engineer shuts it off.

"So?" Jerrod says. "Y'all like it?"

I don't say anything at first. Jerrod already looks so pitiful, I don't want to bring any more bad news.

"I'm sorry, J, but that sucked," Justin says.

We all turn to look at him.

"What did you just say?" Jerrod narrows his eyes.

"It was trash! The track was good. Lyrics were aiight. The delivery is just off, man."

Jerrod frowns. "Now you sound like Destiny."

"Maybe Destiny was just trying to help you get better," I venture. "You know, constructive criticism."

Jerrod rubs his chin, considers this.

"I just have writer's block. The breakup is messing with my flow."

Justin opens his mouth to protest, but Jerrod talks over him.

"Forget it. It's Friday night. My mind isn't right. Let's go to the club."

I'm just about to say that I don't feel like going to the club—I'm not dressed for it anyway, nor do I have the fake ID of the bald-headed man in his forties from Kentucky that Jerrod got for me—when the engineer speaks up.

"If you leave now you forfeit the rest of your studio time." He points to the clock. "You have an hour left."

The prospect of listening to Jerrod rap for an hour is not a good one.

Jerrod snaps his fingers. "Cool. Let's brainstorm. No pressure. Maybe it'll put my rapping back on track."

I doubt this, but I don't mind. I'd never been in a real studio session before. Something deep, deep down inside me was even a little excited about it.

"Sure," I say. Justin glares at me and I shrug. I knew he was going to try to use this as an excuse to leave, but this was payback for telling my parents about Dillie earlier.

Excited, Jerrod hands us two pads with yellow lined paper and two pens.

"Where's yours?" I ask.

"Oh, I don't use one. I'm trying to be like Jay-Z and not write my raps down, you know."

"*Riiiight*," Justin says.

My phone beeps with a text from my parents saying that they were going to bed, and to not forget to turn the porch light off when I get home. I answer it and check all my social media, where I see an eClip from Delia, talking about her latest podcast.

"Speaking of writing," Justin starts. "You need to be working on what you're going to send Delia."

"Delia who? Delia Dawson that goes to y'all's school? Yo, she is *fine*," Jerrod says, looking at Delia over my shoulder. "She does the podcast, right? You're sending in something for that?"

"No, he's sending her a message to ask her out," Justin replies before I can.

"Oh, word?" Jerrod points to my phone. "Well, do it now, so we can see what she says."

I wasn't amused by the possibility of getting rejected in front of these two, but Justin is my best friend and Jerrod was in no shape to diss me if it didn't work out.

I guess there really is no time like the present.

"So what are you going to say?" Justin asks.

I have no idea. Do I tell her how beautiful she is? How talented? Smart? Do I just ask her what she's doing tomorrow? Does she want to see the new Jordan Peele movie?

I click on her profile and the button to message her. I know she likes movies, so I pick the Jordan Peele question.

I type slowly, stopping every few seconds to change words here and there.

But nothing feels right.

Maybe my dad had a point. Dillie's inbox is probably flooded with messages. What would make mine different? What if she glances at it and registers that I asked her out, and the next time I see her in person it's just awkward? When I ask her out, it *has* to be perfect. And this wasn't perfect.

I delete the message and close the app.

"What are you doing?" Justin yells.

I shrug. "It's not the right time. Maybe—maybe I'll send it later," I say, even though I feel pretty confident that I will never send her a Clip Message now.

"Bruh—" Justin starts.

"Let's just listen to these beats." I need to change the subject before Justin lectures me again.

Jerrod sits by the engineer and lets us preview a few tracks. Most are hard-hitting, faster beats, clearly made for rap. Some have that same piano overlay, adding a softer sound. With each song, the bass booms louder through the studio, and Justin, Jerrod, the engineer, and I nod instinctively.

About four tracks later, the beats start to run together.

Justin stands up to stretch, and I suck my teeth. He's about to do his "I'm ready to go" shtick, where he yawns, looks around, says he's tired, then looks at his phone and claims his mom texted him a few minutes ago asking about him. It's always a lie. But I don't call him out on it this time because I'm ready to leave, too.

He's about to yawn when my phone buzzes in my pocket. I pull it out, checking to see where the notification came from.

At first glance, I see the username @dillie_d, and my stomach jolts. I tap the notification and I'm taken to a screen showing Dillie's smiling face.

"Hey, y'all," she says, her eyes flickering back and forth at something she's reading on her screen. I realize that she's streaming live on eClips. "What's up?" she continues. "I thought I'd do a quick LiveClip Q&A before my friends and I go out." Two of her friends, one of them being Mia from earlier, runs to the camera to smile and wave as they put on earrings and secure bobby pins into their hair.

I wonder where they're going? I think. I look around the dimly lit studio. Justin is patting his knee and rapping Jerrod's lyrics back to him, trying to guide him back to the beat. The engineer laughs at some video on his phone that went viral like two months ago. He watches it over and over again. Wherever Dillie's going, I bet it's better than where I am now. I start to daydream about leaving the studio to hang out with her.

Someone must've asked my question to Dillie because she says, "We don't know yet. We heard there was a party we might check out, but Mia wants pizza. Any ideas?"

A bunch of comments fly across the screen, suggesting various pizza parlors and parties in the area. I scramble to name a pizza place that no one's mentioned yet, when I see a comment that makes my stomach flip.

But what about a movie? The new Jordan Peele. Check ur Clip Messages.

Oh no. Immediately, I start to regret not sending a message. Now someone took my idea. Now they are going to go to the movie, start dating, go to prom, become high school sweethearts, and get married, just like my parents.

Her eyes flicker as she reads through each message, mouthing and smiling at each question and comment on the screen.

Until she reads that one.

She squints and simply says, "I don't check my Clip Messages." She scrolls down, reading the next comment after.

My chest deflates like a balloon. Okay, it looks like I made the right call after all.

Justin looks up and laughs. He must've heard her.

"Huh. I guess I was wrong for once. It's time to do something else."

But what?

"I know you didn't ask me, but—" Jerrod starts.

"You're right. I didn't ask you," I mumble, and Justin guffaws, slapping his knee.

Jerrod holds his hands up. "I didn't mean any harm by that, man. I was just saying. Of course a girl like Delia isn't going to be impressed by a Clip Message. Especially since y'all go to the same school. Do you know how many random messages and pictures she must get? People probably do it every day, asking for everything from dates to getting featured on her podcast."

That's exactly what I thought.

"That's true, man." Justin gives me a knowing glance. I'm

annoyed because they are presenting this to me like it's a new idea, like I've never thought of this before. And I can tell Justin is not going to let me get out of asking her that easily.

Jerrod pats his chest. "Aye, I'm just trying to save someone else from the heartbreak that I went through. But before you get in too deep, just make sure she supports your dreams."

"If only you knew how much this man dreams," Justin says. "Look, he's probably dreaming right now."

Justin and Jerrod share a laugh while I flip them a finger my mom wouldn't approve of. I turn my attention back to Dillie's livestream.

"I don't play music on my podcast, so please stop sending me links to your EP," she says, scrolling through the messages. Her eyes get a playful gleam. "Just save it for the contest."

Contest? I turn the volume up on my phone.

A bunch of question marks and comments fly across the screen, asking the question that everyone now wants to know. What contest?

"I shouldn't have said anything so soon." Dillie leans her head back and addresses one of her friends, who says something like, "Just give them a heads-up!"

"Mia thinks I should give you a heads-up. Do y'all agree?" A bunch of smiley faces fly across the screen in unison, viewers anxious to know what she's talking about.

"Okay," Dillie says slowly. She moves closer to the screen, her full lips taking up the frame. "I'm looking for a theme song for my podcast, and I'm holding a contest to find one. The winner's entry will become my theme and they'll be featured on my show."

My heart pounds in my chest. I feel a light bulb turn on somewhere in the back of my head, but I extinguish it before it comes to the surface.

But Justin and Jerrod hear this. "A contest?" Justin says. "Everybody and their grandma is about to enter! You know how many people listen to this podcast?"

This is true. Dillie's show has gained so much traction. My sister even listens to it in college. I've seen more than a few local articles mentioning Dillie's podcast as "The Next Big Thing."

"This is perfect!" says Jerrod. "I can submit a song. Once I win, Destiny will take me back. She listens to Dillie's podcast." He chuckles. "Imagine her getting ready to listen to *Dillie D in the Place to Be* and BOOM"—he slaps his hand for emphasis—"she hears my voice coming through the speakers. She'll believe in me as an artist then."

Justin looks over to me and loudly fake-whispers, "I wonder if he really believes the things that come out of his mouth?"

But Jerrod is motivated. He jumps up and hops back into the booth. "Jack, can you play the tracks of those last three songs, please?"

Jack stops laughing at months-old memes, scoots back up to the control panel, and plays some beats. The first two are way too fast for Jerrod, and much to the approval of Justin's and my ears, he realizes this, as he asks Jack to skip to the final track.

It stops Justin and I in *our* tracks. It's a slow-tempo beat, one that sounds like nineties R&B mixed with a trap sound. There's a synthesizer, and I've never heard anything like it. Jerrod is about to rap over it, but it sounds like someone else should . . . never mind. Forget it.

Justin nods and pounds his fist on the wall, imitating the beat. "Yo, Jerrod this beat is smooth. It sounds like trap music, but mixed with—"

"Jodeci. Right?" I say, taking a page out of the many, *many* nineties R&B songs my parents attempt to play through their Bluetooth speaker.

"Yeah, right in that era!" Justin says.

We listen until Jerrod gets his lyrics together and raps them, off-beat, over the track.

"*Dillie D in the Place to Be* is starting right now so take your seat."

Jerrod's rapping was like a record scratch on a perfect track. Or nails scratching a chalkboard.

He goes for a few verses and comes out of the booth excited.

"I know that was only the first run, but what do y'all think so far?"

The room is quiet.

Jerrod picks up on the awkward silence and tries to double back.

"I mean, the track was something different from what I usually produce—"

"Wait, hold up," I interrupt, holding my hands up. "*You* produced this track?"

"Yeah." Jerrod shrugs. "I produced all of them."

"Bro!" Justin throws his hands up. "This track is *nice*! All of them were! Stop rapping, you suck! Focus on producing!"

He furrows his brow, considering this. "But I don't like to limit myself in my creative endeavors—"

"'Lend to the talent that lends to you,'" I say, quoting my mom. It was how she got my dad to stop messing things up at his office job and focus on becoming a chef, which he excels at.

Jerrod rubs his chin again. "Maybe you're on to something. But I can't just send Dillie D a track with nothing on it."

"Let's brainstorm," Justin says, completely forgoing his "I'm ready to leave" shtick.

For a second, I consider leaving myself, but then I remember Justin drove us here. And as Justin and I scoot closer together, grabbing the pens and yellow notepads, with Jerrod's beats playing in the background, I'm kind of curious about what's going to happen. The energy in the room has changed—I get the feeling that this will be one of those times that mean nothing right now, but later, will mean everything.

The three of us try to brainstorm a way that Jerrod can use his track without his lack of rapping skills poisoning the entire thing.

I drift off into my own thoughts, the yellow paper slowly morphing around me into the dreamworld I've created for myself. We have the track playing on repeat, and the sound of Jerrod steadily trying to rap on beat fades away to the melody I've created for the chorus.

Stop whatever you're doing
Stop whatever you're doing
Dillie D in the Place to Be *is on*
And you better be tuned in

Sundays at 3:00 p.m. keep it locked
Dillie D in your speaker box,
No better podcast in the world
And Dillie D, you're my favorite girl

I hum the melody, scribbling down the words faster than they were coming to me. As the track loops, I repeat the lyrics again, trying a different arrangement. I want to write more, but I'm stuck on what I should say. What I *want* to say. I haven't felt this way since my last performance, when everything changed and I decided to quit singing for good. Except this time, there's no embarrassing performance or jeers involved. Just me and my words. The light bulb in my head is shining brighter and brighter, no matter how hard I try to dim it. It feels good.

The track stops playing. I wait for it to loop again, and it doesn't.

I look up, and find Justin, Jerrod, and even Jack staring at me, their mouths open.

"What?" I ask, raising my eyebrow. "What are y'all looking at?"

"You!" Justin says, slowly getting up, pointing at me and

walking toward me. "You—you can *sing*! Like, I knew you sung in choir, but you can actually *sing* sing. Like, you can *sang*."

I turn away from the three of them and back to the legal pad. But it feels different now. The song is not in my head anymore. It's out in the open, for the world to see. I feel exposed.

They are still staring at me.

"Darren, all this time you could've been singing your feelings to Delia! Pure talent!" Jerrod says. "You're like the next Usher . . . or . . ."

"Nah, not Usher. Darren's not a dancer." Justin looks at me and narrows his eyes. "Or *are* you? What other talents are you hiding from us?"

"I'm not hiding anything," I say, defensively. "I used to sing at church and in the school chorus. You know that."

"Well . . . well, I'm saying, maybe you can do both. Sing for church and school, and also sing songs begging for the love of your life."

"I'm not singing anything," I say, getting annoyed now. "I was just . . . messing around." The light bulb in my head flickers. My stomach flips. It felt good for a second, but I'm not a singer anymore. I *can't*.

"Darren, we *heard* you," Jerrod says, punching his palm into his hand. "Us artists need to stick together. Think about it— maybe I can take a break from rapping and focus on producing, and you sing. Your voice and melodies will be perfect over tracks like that. We'll blow up in no time! Then, once I'm established as a producer, I can go back to rapping—"

"I think you should consider this just for the fact that Jerrod said he'd take a break from rapping," Justin cuts in.

Justin and Jerrod go back and forth on what I should do, and I let them. At first, I'm a little flattered that they actually think my singing voice is *that* good. But then it gets annoying. Because I know after what happened, it's not true. And I don't like that they're talking about me like I'm not even there. Whatever. Keeps the attention off my song.

Until Justin snaps his fingers, cutting Jerrod off, and looks at me. "Darren. We've been playing this all wrong. If you send this in to Dillie's contest, *you* could win."

Jerrod looks at me like this is the most obvious and best idea, but I shake my head at both of them.

"No. I'm not one of those guys trying to hustle their music." I imagine myself working day and night on a song and hounding others to listen to it, only for them to turn their noses up at me and my songs go unheard. No thanks.

"So, you just want to sing to yourself?"

What's wrong with that? If I mess up, it won't be a big deal. Nobody will film it, comment on it, or critique it.

I say nothing though, just shrug.

"The only thing is, it's too slow, she'll fall asleep listening to it like this," Jerrod says, scrolling through his laptop.

"I like it the way it is," I say, then I shake my head. What does it matter? I'm not going to send it in anyway.

"She needs an upbeat song," Jerrod says. "Let's do this one."

He clicks a few buttons and lands on a fast-tempo beat. Jerrod is good at what he does as far as producing, but I don't like this track as much. It doesn't match as well with the lyrics. With the first beat, the bass moved in and out, emphasizing certain words. This new one doesn't have any bass at all, it seems like. It's too fast for the lyrics and changes the entire vibe that I had in my head.

"*Yeah!*" Justin says, nodding to the beat. "It'll sound much better this way! The other one was good, but kind of dull."

I furrow my brow. Dull? I didn't think it was dull at all. I thought it was smooth and different.

"Sing it again and let's see," Jerrod says.

I take a deep breath, sigh, and sing part of the song again. I sing it faster, to stay on beat with the new track. When I finish, it almost makes me hate what I wrote. The track doesn't mesh well with my voice at all.

But Justin and Jerrod grin and nod.

"You'd definitely win with this," Jerrod says.

"No" is all I say. I hate the track, but again, it's not like I'm going to submit it. I'm reminded of one of the reasons I stopped singing—the unwanted opinions—and the light bulb in my head flickers off.

"Your loss. The faster one seems like an easy way to—" Justin's phone rings. "Hold up, y'all. It's Tiffany."

We listen awkwardly as Tiffany says something on the phone, and Justin blushes and says something back in his fake deep voice.

"Yo, get a room!" Jerrod says, frowning. Poor guy. Probably upset that he and his girlfriend are on the outs.

I look down at the yellow legal pad holding the words I wrote about Dillie. I think about how Jerrod, though broken up with his girlfriend and heartbroken about it, still gave it a shot. And Justin, who is Off Again with Tiffany every other week, still answers the phone and puts on his deep voice every time she calls.

All I have right now with Dillie are thoughts—not even real memories. Thoughts with a real person who's living her real life, probably eating pizza, right this very second.

"All right, Darren. You ready?" Justin asks, shoving his phone into his pocket and looking at me. He's ready to go, finally. Either he's going to make a pit stop at Tiffany's house or he wants to go home and use his fake deep voice on the phone with her in peace.

I look down at the legal pad again. I pick it up, just so my words won't hang around this studio for the world, or at least my small part of it, to see.

"Yeah. I'm ready."

05: Chorus & Crepes

I wake up the next day to my phone vibrating on my nightstand, rattling until it eventually falls off. As much as I try to ignore the call, it keeps ringing, which means it can be only one person.

My sister.

I sigh and pick up my phone, which greets me with a picture of my sister and me at her high school graduation. I answer it.

"Hey—" I start.

"*Hiiii*, baby brother!!" I see my sister's face as she yells into the phone. She's loud for no reason, like Dad.

"What's up, Zoe," I say, rubbing what my mom calls the "coal" out of my eyes.

"Eww. Wipe the coal from your eyes," she says.

"That's what I'm doing," I mumble, rolling over. She's already up, dressed, and in the passenger seat of a car. "What are you doing up this early?" I ask.

"Going to brunch." Zoe is in her freshman year of college in Georgia. She's majoring in broadcast journalism and wants to be the next Oprah. I have no doubt that she will. She loves to talk and is able to get the truth from people easily like Mom. That is, when she's not listening to the sound of her own voice first.

"Should I get pancakes or waffles?" she asks offhandedly to me and whoever is driving. Zoe always does this. Asks for advice for small things that really don't matter to the rest of us.

But she'll bug me if I don't choose one, so I answer anyway. "Pancakes," I respond, right when someone with a deeper voice says, "Waffles."

I frown. "Who said that?" I ask, sitting up in bed, trying to look tough. It's hard, though, because I have on a faded Spider-Man shirt. Spider-Man was my favorite superhero growing up, and this is the most comfortable sleep shirt I own.

Zoe blushes a bit, then pans the camera quickly over to whoever is driving. Some guy with a full beard.

"This is Brandon."

Brandon quickly glances over at the phone and does a quick two-finger salute. "What's up, bro?"

I am not his bro.

"Zoe—" I start. I don't want to be rude to her company, but who is this man saluting me while I'm in my Spider-Man sleep shirt?

"Don't tell Dad yet," Zoe says. Dad isn't mean to Zoe's boyfriends, but of course he is embarrassing to no end.

"You'll be able to meet Brandon soon. I'm coming back for homecoming."

"Word?" I say.

Zoe was one of those people who was heard about before she was seen, which is saying something, because she was seen everywhere. She did the announcements every single morning when she was in high school, along with student government, yearbook, and, for a brief stint, cheerleading, which she quit after she tore her ACL. She decided she didn't love it enough to continue after she recovered.

Most people would think it was tough to be in Zoe's shadow, but I didn't mind. It meant I didn't have to talk much, and people felt like they knew me enough to not ask too many questions.

"Yup. So . . . I'll tell Dad about Brandon then."

"You're going to surprise him?" I ask, raising my eyebrow. This didn't sound like a great idea.

"Yeah . . . anyway, what are you up to? What do you have planned today?"

"Nothing really. It's Saturday."

"Meeting up with friends?"

"Maybe later."

"Girlfriend?"

"I—huh?"

Zoe laughs. "I just wanted to see what you were going to say. No girlfriend? Or do you just not want to tell big sis?"

Brandon laughs at that, which annoys me. This is a conversation between my sister and me, and not some college guy with a huge beard.

"Nah. I—I don't have a girlfriend." For all the thoughts in

the world I have about Dillie, we aren't even close to being together.

"You sure?" Zoe says, raising her own eyebrow, my face briefly reflected in hers. "You didn't look so confident in that answer. You dating someone?"

"Is that my Zoe?" My mom opens my bedroom door with a laundry basket in her hands.

"Yes," I say as Mom puts the basket on my desk chair, squeezes onto my bed, pushes her face against mine, and starts squealing. "Hey, Zoe!"

Zoe grins back with a smile identical to Mom's. "Hey, Ma! I was just asking Darren about his love life."

I frown. *Really, Zoe?* After you've sworn me to secrecy about your *own* love life?

But Mom perks up at this. "Love life? You talking about the cute girl from church? Did you ask her out yet?"

This cannot be happening. "Come on, Mom." I groan.

"Wait, what cute girl from church?" Zoe asks. She and Brandon have finally gotten to their destination and are getting out of the car.

"Delia, right?" Mom looks at me for fake confirmation. She knows the answer is yes. I say nothing because I know the conversation will continue even if I don't contribute.

"Delia Dawson? The girl with the podcast? Aiming high, huh, D? Girls in my dorm listen to that podcast every Sunday night when they twist their hair. It's so popular here."

"Aiming *high*?" my mom asks, folding her arms. "They would complement each other very nicely. Darren is nice and smart. A true gentleman."

Leave it to Mom to hype me up.

"Of course! I was just saying she's popular, ambitious, and pretty. I'm sure a lot of people try to get her attention every day," Zoe says.

I think back to the studio, where Jerrod and Justin pretty much said the exact same thing. As much as they collectively sound like a broken record, it's all true.

"Well, none of them are my Darren. Right, sweetie?" my mom asks. I give a noncommittal half nod, half shrug.

"You're right, Ma. So Darren, did you ask her out yet?"

It takes a second for me to realize that Zoe wants *me* to answer this question, but before I can, I see another arm reach out for the phone and take it.

Brandon's face appears. "Let me school you, young buck."

"*School* me?" I blurt out, not able to hold in my annoyance any longer. "School *me* on *what*?"

"When there are a lot of men striving for the attention of one girl, you have to set yourself apart," he says, walking across a parking lot with my sister's phone, then opening the door for her to enter what looks like a restaurant.

"Set yourself apart," he repeats. "Show what you can bring to the table, and how you can add value to her life."

"Zoe?" my mom asks, with an air of both confusion and intrigue in her voice. "Zoe? Who is this young man?"

"What young man?" I hear another voice come from my bedroom door. Dad's.

"Come and see, Dad." I wave him over, getting my revenge on Zoe for telling Mom about my nonexistent love life.

There's a lot of muffled noise and movement, then Zoe takes the phone back.

"Gotta go, y'all! Our table is ready! See y'all soon. Kiss kiss!" The phone call disconnects.

"What young man?" Dad asks.

Mom looks at me, eager to know. Telling Mom is like telling Dad.

"Nobody. I think she's meeting up with a group of friends."

"Oh," Dad says. "Well, come on downstairs, I gotta new crepe recipe that I want you to try."

When Dad said he had a new crepe recipe he wanted me to try, I thought he meant tasting the crepes, not actually *cooking* them. I'm an okay cook, nowhere near as good as Mom or Dad, and I definitely do the bare minimum when it comes to breakfast. Yet, here I am, in the kitchen with Dad, making crepes.

"Pass me the flour, son," he says as he reads some notes from a tablet with a bunch of scribbled-out and rewritten words on it. It reminds me of the tablet I used at Incredible Beatz. Maybe cooking is like songwriting. Scribbled-out words, trial and error, something sweet at the end.

Hopefully, Dad doesn't ruin this crepe recipe with chopped onions or something the way Jerrod and Justin ruined my song with that track.

We talk a little bit as I pass him the flour tin and crack and whisk some eggs. I catch myself humming the song I wrote and stop when Dad looks at me.

"Tune in your head?" He mixes the flour with sugar and a little bit of salt. My parents will latch on to any opening to talk about me singing. Carefully, though, because they don't want to push me away. Again.

I nod. "Just a little . . ." I was going to say "something I wrote," but I stop. I don't want to get his hopes up.

Dad mixes his ingredients. "That's all you used to do when you were a baby, you know. You couldn't even talk yet. You'd always hum or babble to some tune. Your mother and I would be out and someone would say, 'You have a little singer on your hands.' That was always your thing."

He's told me this before, but somehow, the words settle differently. *That was always my thing.* It was. When I was sad? I would sing. Happy? I would sing. Upset because my parents grounded me? I'd write a song about it and whisper-sing it in my room. Yeah, I know. Kind of embarrassing.

When I couldn't find the words, or really didn't want to say anything, I could sing and people would get what I was trying to say.

Not now, though. I guess I don't really have a "thing" anymore.

"Yeah." I pour the eggs into Dad's mixing bowl. "Especially when we realized Zoe couldn't."

We laugh at that. Zoe, who excels at virtually everything, can't hold a note to save her life. I didn't start singing because of that, but it was a nice bonus to have something of my own. Until Zoe, in true Zoe fashion, started telling me when and what to sing, when we'd play together as kids and even when I got a little older.

"So." Dad lowers his voice. "Really, who was the young man Zoe was talking to on the phone?"

I just shrug, adding milk to the bowl. I told her I wouldn't tell Dad. I'd usually be grateful to have a distraction—that means no questions about Dillie and no not-so-subtle questions about singing. Now it feels different. The conversation about Zoe doesn't feel like a relief, but a little out of place. I think Dad feels it too because we're silent as he mixes everything together.

"You know, son," Dad says as he flips the crepes in the pan. "Out of me and all seven of your aunts and uncles, I'm the only one that truly inherited Grandma's cooking gene."

"Way to be modest, Dad," I say as a sweet aroma fills the kitchen. My stomach rumbles in response.

"Oh no, son, I'm not bragging," he says. "I'm not a bragger.

I'm like you in that way. I remember one Thanksgiving I thought my pie was going to be so good, better than Grandma's, so I purposely left it in the oven a little bit longer to crisp it up."

I furrow my brow. "Why would you do that?"

"Ah, I don't know. I guess I was afraid to consider that I really was the best. Think about the pressure—the best sweet potato pie at Thanksgiving with seven brothers and sisters? Whew!" He takes the pan and flips the crepes perfectly onto the plate, then adds a few berries on top. "The funny thing is, it was still the best pie and everyone knew it. Imagine how much better it would've been had I took it out the oven on time, instead of purposely sabotaging my pie."

"Did you take it out on time during the next Thanksgiving?" I ask, handing Dad more plates for the rest of his crepes.

"Yup. And it was still the best. I didn't even have to say a word. Everybody knew."

Dad hands me his first crepe.

"How does it taste?"

I take a bite.

"This is good, Dad."

"Thanks, son."

"You really do your thing in the kitchen."

Dad smiles. "Yeah, yeah. I know I do," he says playfully. "Tell your mother that breakfast is ready."

06: Unreleased

Dillie D in the Place to Be airs every Sunday afternoon at 3:00. It's that small time after church, but before dinner, when everyone is prepping for the week or napping. It's genius because I can listen to it in my room uninterrupted. Like Zoe said, girls can twist and style their hair for the week while they listen. And whatever she talks about stays fresh to be discussed at school on Monday morning.

I drive to church in the morning and leave after my parents do, as Mom is helping out with children's church and Dad is having a meeting in the church kitchen to discuss the menu for Wednesday night dinners this month. I help out, too, but since I don't sing anymore, I don't have to stay after as late. I know it bugs my parents that I don't stick around for choir practice. I can practically see the question forming around their heads when we see the choir director after church, or when one of the worship songs I used to sing comes on the radio on the way home. But I'm sure they know that all the questions is one of the reasons I quit in the first place.

We eat dinner pretty early on Sundays, and I'm welcomed by

the aroma of it, slow cooking in the kitchen when I walk back into the house. I change out of my church clothes into sweatpants and a random T-shirt (not the Spider-Man one), lie down, and scroll through my phone until it's time for Dillie's podcast.

I'm in the mood for music.

I reach for my Bluetooth speaker and realize I forgot to charge it last night. I run downstairs to get my parents' speaker, run back up, and plug it in.

"Turn it on," I say. "My Heart Belongs To U" blares from the speaker, and I chuckle as I reach to turn it off. My parents will *never* stop listening to nineties hip-hop and R&B. I catch some of the words and hum to them, thinking of Dillie.

I hum the chorus along with Jodeci, easily finding the harmony in between them all. This song is a lot more relatable than I thought. I let my parents' playlist play, a mixture of soul, new jack swing, and R&B.

My alarm buzzes. 3:00 p.m. Time for Dillie's show.

I open up my podcast app and tap the newest episode without even reading the description.

"It's *Dillie D in the Place to Be*." Delia's voice comes through the speaker, a simple jingle to start off her new show.

"What's up, y'all, it's Dillie," she says as the tiny bit of background music fades away. "I have quite an interesting show for you today. We've already been getting *so* many submissions for the theme song contest I mentioned on my LiveClip, and I didn't even officially announce it on my show yet. One of them is . . .

particularly mysterious to say the least, but in a good way. We'll get into them a little later on.

"For those of you who don't know, I'm hosting a contest to find a new theme song for my podcast. At this point, I'm tired of hearing my own voice say, 'It's *Dillie D in the Place to Be*' every Sunday. I want a real song that makes people excited to listen. I'll be accepting submissions through the end of next Friday, so walk, don't run, to your nearest studio and send me your best work! I'll announce the winner on my show two weeks from today!

"I wanted to start off by giving you a little taste of the competition. You know, just to see who the rest of y'all are up against. I picked out a couple of my favorites, and like I said, a super interesting one. Hit me up on eClips—I'm @dillie_d there—and let me know what you think! Okay, let's start with my first favorite new submission."

Dillie's voice fades out and a song fades in. It's catchy, and I nod to the beat.

But the lyrics suck. It's just two dudes saying "Dillie D" over and over again, getting louder and louder each time.

The song fades out. "Y'all have to admit, that was kind of catchy! Okay, here's another one I like."

This time it's a girl's voice. It sounds familiar. This track is a lot slower, a neo-soul beat like something Erykah Badu would sing over. There's a bit of spoken word at the end. It's a nice concept, but I don't think it fits the vibe of Dillie's show.

"I appreciate y'all's creativity!" Dillie says after the poem is over. "Here's another one."

This time it's a guy's voice, singing. He has good tone, and good lyrics, but no voice control. He tries to cover it up with lots of vibrato, but from years of singing in church, I knew that singing loud with vibrato a good singer does not always make.

I always feel weird sitting back and critiquing other people's singing. Especially since I don't sing anymore. I didn't even submit anything to this contest. At least this guy was trying.

I start to feel the call of the sweet Sunday nap. This happens sometimes when I listen to Dillie's show, and when it does I just finish listening to the rest later that night. Her voice comes back on after the guy's song fades out, but I'm suddenly too sleepy to pay attention.

> *Stop whatever you're doing*
> *Stop whatever you're doing*
> Dillie D in the Place to Be *is on*
> *And you better be tuned in*

I open my eyes just as I start to dream about the song I wrote for Dillie.

It's still playing. My thoughts are never *this* loud.

It takes me a second to realize it's coming from the speaker.

I listen as the muffled sound of my voice blares throughout my room over the slow track that Jerrod produced.

My heart is racing. I scrub my eyes, confused. What's going on?

"I love this one!" Dillie says as my voice fades out. "It was sent anonymously and so mysterious. Was someone in the process of working on the song and decided to give a sneak peek? Whoever it was, they can *sang*. I hope they send a finished version soon.

"Those are all of the submissions from this week. Now on to this week's topic. The new Jordan Peele movie . . ."

Although I feel a tiny pang of regret because I didn't ask her to see the movie with me before she discussed it on her show, I can't think about it yet because I'm already out of bed, grabbing my keys, slipping on my shoes and sweatpants, and heading out the door.

As I'm pulling into Justin's driveway, a car is pulling out, and honks at me on the way down the street. It's his girlfriend, Tiffany. I give her a quick salute and park.

It takes everything in me not to bang on Justin's door. But I don't want to upset his mom.

I knock curtly. He opens the door and is surprised to see me there.

"What's up?" he whispers, taking in the anger in my face.

"Bruh—" I start.

"Shh," he whispers again. "My parents fell asleep on the couch. Just come up to my room, Jerrod is up there."

Both Justin's parents are cuddled on the couch, fast asleep with the TV on. The smell of corn bread hits my nose and my stomach growls.

We walk upstairs, where Jerrod is in a desk chair doing something on Justin's computer. Justin shuts the door.

"What's up?" Justin asks again.

"Bruh! Which one of y'all recorded me singing that Dillie D
song and sent it to her show? Don't lie, I just heard it today." I
feel exposed, like my personal journal is out for the world to see.

Justin holds up his hands. "It wasn't me. For real. I wouldn't
do that—*I* at least would've had you record it in the studio before
I sent it off secretly."

I narrow my eyes. He's not helping his case.

"Justin—"

"I did it."

We both look over at Jerrod. He shrugs.

"I sent it to her." He is nonchalant as he returns to his beats.

Justin's eyes are wide. "You did?"

"Jerrod, why would you do that?" I'm wondering how quietly I
can punch Jerrod without Justin's parents waking up. Even though
I'm usually not a fighter.

He shrugs again. "Look. I know I appear tough, but I'm just a
hopeless romantic, trying to save your love life, man." He holds
his tattooed hands to his heart.

Justin scoffs. "You actually don't appear tough. Like, at all."

"After what happened with me and my girl, I couldn't let a
potential new love just fizzle out. You were never going to get in
the studio and record that song alone. I knew if Dillie heard a piece

of it she'd want to hear the real thing and that would inspire you to get back in the booth. I have a real ear for talent, you know."

"Well, can you hear what *you* sound like?" Justin smirks, trying to lighten the mood. I'm still pissed.

Jerrod nods. "Of course. I just *said* I have an ear for talent."

I shake my head. Can they focus? "What did you send? Did you tell her it was me?"

"Nope. I said it's an anonymous singer-slash-admirer."

I groan. "You told her I was an admirer?" I run my hand across my face.

Jerrod looks surprised at my anger. "Well, yeah. I mean, wasn't it obvious with the lyrics? You said she was your favorite girl."

"How did you even do that? Did you make up a fake email address or something?"

"Yeah—MysterySinger@ClipMail.com." Jerrod types something into the computer and an email inbox comes up. "See? The password is DarrenArmstrong. So obvious, she'll never guess!"

The inbox is empty, meaning she didn't respond yet.

I still can't believe she's heard it. I just stand there, staring at Jerrod.

"I would've sent in the better version, you know, the party version we made. But I forgot to record you singing that one. She can at least get the gist with this one. Maybe we can rerecord it later." He grins, clearly pleased with himself.

I still can't believe that she's heard it. *Any* version of it.

"So, when are you going to go to the booth and finish?" Jerrod prompts. "We need to hurry."

"Who said I was?"

Justin eyes me incredulously. "Okay, Darren. I know you're upset that Jerrod sent Dillie the recording but . . . I mean, this is perfect, right? The way to let Dillie know you like her just fell into your lap." This gives me the mental image of my dad supposedly falling into my mom's lap decades ago.

"All you have to do now is tell her that that was you," Justin continues.

"No," I say. "I know I was supposed to tell her how I feel but . . . not like this."

"Then how?" Justin asks.

I don't know, but not like this.

"You can't see it now, Darren," Jerrod says. "But opportunity is knocking, and you better answer it."

A knock at the door makes the three of us jump.

"Well, I guess my name is Opportunity." Justin's mom peeks her head in. "Dinner's ready. Crockpot roast and veggies. Darren, you're welcome to stay."

07: Song Credits

"You really don't think anyone will recognize it was me singing?" I ask Justin as we walk across campus Monday morning.

Justin nods, adjusting his book bag on his back. "Bruh, no one even knows you *can* sing like that. I doubt someone will put two and two together."

We greet our friends and no one looks at me for a second too long or with a knowing glance. I don't know if it's because this makes Justin right—and I hate when Justin is right—but it doesn't sit right with *me*.

"It's weird that you don't want people to know. I mean, I knew you were in chorus but I thought that was just because you needed an elective or something. And everyone sings in church choir. You clearly have this talent and you don't want anyone to know. Why?"

He looks over at me, waiting for an answer, but I pretend I don't hear him and veer sharply left on the way to my locker, telling him I'll see him at lunch. It's hard to explain, especially right before homeroom.

While Justin heads to class and I keep walking a little farther to my locker, I'm playing out the idea that I *do* go to the studio and rerecord the song. The possibility that I win the contest and do the interview, and from there, what? Everything could spiral out of control. My dreamworld would be open for the real world to see. And everyone would walk in uninvited with their opinions and critiques. But at least I'd be singing again. Was that a good thing?

"Darren?"

I glance up, directly into the brown eyes of Dillie. She has the essence of a smile on her face—like she'd just finished laughing not too long ago or she's thinking about something amusing.

"Oh—hey, Dillie," I say. "What's up?" I realize we're in front of my locker. She must've stopped on her way to her class. None of her friends are around.

If there ever was a perfect time to tell her how I feel, this would be it.

"Are you okay?" She clutches the books and notebook in her arms. "You look like you're thinking about something serious."

"Oh, nah." I open my locker and grab my own books and notebooks. "I'm just—in my own head a lot."

Why would I say that? *Why?*

"Yeah, I know the feeling," Dillie says. "I know it seems like I'm always talking outside my head." She laughs. "But I'm always thinking about something behind the scenes."

"Same here," I say. "Not the talking-outside-of-my-head part. More like inside my head. I'm always thinking of something behind the scenes, too."

Shut *up*, Darren.

"Are you going to the lock-in at church this weekend?" she asks, adjusting the straps on her book bag.

"Yeah..." I trail off. I've been going to the youth lock-in every year since I was in the sixth grade, and I was starting to feel just a little too old for it. I would ask Justin to come, to guarantee I wouldn't be the only junior there, but it's only for members of our church.

"Oh, it's going to be so fun," Dillie says.

"Wait. You're going?"

She nods. "I love interacting with the middle school girls, seeing everyone show off their talents that we don't get to see during the Sunday service."

She leans in closer and lowers her voice. My heart pounds against my chest. "I want to start a mentoring program next summer, and this will be a good way to get in their heads."

I smile, despite myself. Dillie will be there, too. Beautiful, driven, and compassionate.

Suddenly, I can't wait until this lock-in.

"That's what's up. I know they'll love that. They look up to you—they see you as a celebrity because of your podcast. But I guess you are a... local celebrity." I stop myself before I continue babbling.

Her eyes sparkle. "I might as well use that to their advantage to help. Maybe I can inspire them to do something they love."

Her words take me back to what Mrs. Thompson said in our meeting. Could I potentially do the same thing if I start singing again? What if I start right now, by admitting that I'm the mystery singer?

Someone slamming their locker takes me out of my head, and I see Dillie eyeing me curiously.

There has to be something I can say. Should I mention the song?

"How's the contest coming?" I try this out, swirl it around my mouth, see if it feels right. "I heard some of the tracks . . . a few of them were really nice. Do you have a favorite?"

"I'm not sure . . ." She trails off and bites her lip. "Sometimes I feel like I do and sometimes I feel like there's a better submission coming."

"Oh, really?" I say, as casually as possible. I close my locker. I start to walk to class, but I wonder if she'd take it as me walking away from her instead of an invitation to walk with me, so I just stand there.

"Well, I do have *one* favorite," Dillie admits. "But it's hard to say, especially because—"

The first bell rings.

"Oh, shoot," Dillie says. "My next class is in the S building. I'm about to be late. I'll catch you later!"

She jogs away. The students part ways for her to run down the hallway and out the building. She waves at the ones who wave at her, who watch her run just like I do.

I'm at home in my room looking over notes for math class when Justin sends me a text with a link and the message:

Justin: Tiffany is here and she was watching this. We need to go to the studio ASAP!

I click on the link. It's Dillie's profile, a video where she apparently did another Q&A. How did I miss it?

"I decided to do an impromptu Q and A since I'm waiting on my food," she says while walking. She pans the camera over to the neon sign across from her: Andy's Burger Joint. I suck my teeth. Andy's has the worst burgers and he's a little racist. When Justin, Jerrod, and I used to go there to eat he'd always accuse us of trying to steal extra plasticware and remind us to tip. But he'd ignore the other kids from the school down the road who *did* steal the plasticware and "forget" to tip.

Sally's is much better and most people don't know about it, which is another bonus. I consider telling Dillie about it until I realize this is a replay. Not real time.

People are asking Dillie different questions: her favorite TV show at the moment, favorite type of pizza (chicken and banana peppers), where she got her earrings. Then I see a question from a guy in my English class scroll across the screen. Miles.

"You gotta boyfriend, ma?"

I register when Dillie reads the message and she gives a light chuckle.

"Not at the moment," she says. She taps her finger to her chin. "But . . . I'm open to it."

Miles is the guy in class who likes being the center of attention.

He likes a lot of hype around him, but he doesn't really do anything worthy of being hyped up. Not to mention the time he stole my solo when I was still in the school chorus. Well, he didn't exactly steal it. But I had a solo and I put my own spin on it, which our chorus director loved. I added an extra run when there wasn't one (which was a bold move since Mr. Drummond hated too many riffs and runs). When I left chorus, Miles got the solo and would do that exact same spin . . . every time he performed it.

He talks about himself and what he's doing or going to do a lot, so people see him as ambitious. He's the type to announce that he's "moving in silence" toward some goal, which is not exactly a silent thing to do. I see through all of it, but I don't say anything so people don't just think I'm being a hater. I had no idea Miles was interested in Dillie. I mean, I knew I wasn't the only one, but still . . .

She answers a few more questions (ranch or blue cheese, favorite Beyoncé song, something about the shape of her nails) when another someone asks her about the mystery singer, and whether she figured out who sent her the song yet.

"I haven't! But you know what's funny? I was going to talk about this on the show, but I'll give y'all a heads-up—a *lot* of people have actually been coming forward saying it's their song. And I know it's not!"

I frown.

What?

"It's so funny," she continues, chuckling again. "One person came forward, and he *kind of* sounded like the guy in the original recording, but he was singing a different song. He didn't sound as good, so I thought that the studio recording was just showing his true voice. I was like 'Dang, I knew it was too good to be true.'"

But it's not! I want to say. *It's not! I really sound like that!*

"I was still going to have this dude as the top contender because I liked that little recording *so* much. But then, a few hours later, another guy came forward and said it was *his* song! And get this, y'all—of course, by this time, I'm skeptical, so I just ask him to sing on the spot, on the phone. He should sound just like the recording, right? Well, just when I start to believe him, he gets the words to his 'own' song wrong!"

My vision feels like it's blurring as the other viewers of the livestream send Dillie a bunch of laughing emojis and comments.

She snorts a bit, her nose wrinkling at the top as she continues. "Yes! He said, 'Dillie D, it's your world,' and I'm almost certain the original song said, 'Dillie D, you're my favorite girl' because I love that line. But maybe I'm wrong."

You're not, though!

"Either way, I'm skeptical of both of them now and the mystery continues. If I can't confirm the real singer's real submission, though, I'll move on to the next person," she says. She starts reading another question and is interrupted when her name is called.

"Oh, that's my food, y'all. See ya! Don't forget to tune in next Sunday to *Dillie D in the Place to Be* to find out who won the contest!" The video ends.

I stare at the blank screen for a second. Who are these people trying to claim my song? And *why*?

My song.

I glance over to the yellow legal pad I "borrowed" from Incredible Beatz. The scribbled words of the hook are there. Unfinished. I think of someone singing those words to the person I was singing about, acting as me, claiming my music. It makes my stomach flip. I think about what Mrs. Thompson said and how I should shake things up. And Dad's burnt sweet potato pie.

I pick up the legal pad and flip the page over, the blank lines calming my thoughts. Until the only thing I hear is the melody in my head, words flowing out of my mind, through the pen, and onto the page.

08: Rockin' Lock-In

I turn down the old Usher song I'm listening to as I enter the church parking lot and smile unassumingly at a few of the elders leaving their weekly meeting. I won't make the same mistake I made this time last year, when I was blasting an old Notorious B.I.G. song in the parking lot and one of the elders called my parents to tell them how scandalized they were.

I park and start taking some of the dishes out of the back seat. Dad wasn't coming to the lock-in, but he made desserts and sent them with me. A few middle-school-aged boys race past my car and into the student center. I sigh. I hope tonight goes well.

I'm still humming the Usher song when I get a sudden whiff of vanilla. Is it the cake I'm holding?

"Need some help?"

I bang my head against the top of my car as I pull the platter of cake out. I scrunch my face up to avoid crying out in pain, then take a deep breath before I turn around and face Dillie.

"Mmm, cake! I was hoping your dad was cooking today!"

Her coils are piled on top of her head, and she has on a lavender sweat suit, furry boots, and a small book bag on her back.

Since this is technically a glorified slumber party (pun intended), everyone has on some sort of athleisure, including me, in my black tracksuit.

"Yeah. He was upset that we decided to order pizza again this year, but he couldn't pass up the opportunity to make *something*," I say as I try to balance another platter, this time of brownies, in my hands.

Dillie laughs. "Let me grab that."

She takes the cake out of my hands while I grab a small container of chocolate chip cookies. I realize the vanilla scent is coming from her, a sweet smell that I could get used to.

"Thanks," I say, still performing a balancing act as I take my keys out of my pocket and lock my car.

"Are you excited for tonight?"

I hesitate. I played potential scenarios of how the lock-in could go in my head last night and all I could come up with was the same things we always do—pizza from the chain restaurant around the corner, a movie I've seen a million times, ice cream that's slightly melted.

But I look at Dillie, and she looks bright-eyed and excited about tonight, like she knows something I don't. Then I wonder—*does* she? Can she hear it in my voice, that I'm the one who sent in that song? Will she be able to figure it out tonight?

"I don't know," I say, breaking the silence. "It's always cool, but I've done this so many times."

"Well, you haven't done it this time. It could be a lot different."

"Hm. I guess you're right." It would be nice, but I don't count on it.

We walk up to the sign that says "Check-in" and I see the smiling face of one of our church members, Samantha.

"Hi!" she says. "Darren Armstrong, right? And Delia Dawson?" She scans the list quickly and puts a check mark by both our names. "Awesome! You can pin this name tag to your bag and put them over there, and this one to your shirts!" She hands us two name tags each. We both quickly set the desserts down and do this.

"I'm just going to run these desserts over to the kitchen," I say.

Samantha nods enthusiastically and waves. "Thanks, Darren and Delia. And welcome to our annual lock-in!"

I smile at Samantha as I make my way to the kitchen, Dillie walking beside me with the cake.

"Well, well! If it isn't Wyatt's little boy!"

I smile again as we approach the kitchen window and I pass Mr. Wilson, one of the caretakers at our church, the platter of brownies and container of cookies.

"Hi, Mr. Wilson," I say.

"And how you doing, Delia?" He takes the cake from her and they chat a little bit, then turns back to me. "I see Wyatt is still sending up food. I told him we were having pizza tonight!"

"You know my dad" is all I say.

"Look at—that's Zoe's little brother! I swear, you're looking more and more like Zoe every day, but with Dorothea's big brown eyes!"

The woman who says this, Mrs. Rochester, comes out from the kitchen to give Dillie and me a bear hug.

"Delia, how's your show going?"

Dillie giggles and she and Mrs. Rochester briefly chat about the show, with Mr. Wilson joining in. I laugh at their jokes and stand around awkwardly. They aren't talking to me anymore, but it would be rude to leave her since she brought the cake over here.

Mr. Wilson turns to look at me. "Darren, you singing tonight? We sure do miss that voice of yours around here."

I look at him, confused. "Oh, I'm not in the youth choir anymore." I thought maybe he knew that already, but maybe he didn't realize.

"No, not in the *choir* . . ." He trails off as a doorbell rings back in the kitchen. "Oh, that must be the pizza. Well, anyway, Darren, let me know if you do!"

I look at Dillie and shrug. That was weird. Was I just supposed to break out in song during the lock-in?

Maybe *he* knows I'm the mystery singer.

We make our way back through the student center, to a large room where kids and teens of various ages are sitting around, and it's just as I thought.

"Looks like we're the oldest ones here who aren't chaperones," Dillie says as I scan the room for a place to sit.

"I knew this would happen," I say, but I like this feeling. That we are a unit.

She links her arm through mine, and the touch makes my

body warm. "Looks like we have to stick together." I rub my face to hide my blush.

We make our way to a table in the back, where a handful of girls and boys are clustered at one end of it. A few of the girls shush each other and one of them says, "Hey, Dillie!" She waves and Dillie waves back.

"Dillie, you found your mystery singer yet?" I hear someone say.

I freeze. Oh no. Someone knows. What should I say? Should I deny it, or just come clean?

"Because I can sing just as good." A middle-school-aged boy stands up and breaks out in song, his voice cracking every few words. The girls giggle and tell him to shut up and sit down. He does so with a huge grin on his face. I laugh a little, relieved. Of course no one knew it was me. They were just joking. But it does remind me of how big this whole mystery is, and how my song is at the center of it.

"Not yet, but you're right. You sound just like him." Dillie turns away and he grins. Another one of the boys at the table daps him up.

"Does this happen often?" I say. "I'm not used to hanging around a celebrity."

Dillie playfully shoves me. "Stop it. I am glad to know they listen to my show, though. I really do want to provide something for the kids to listen to that makes them laugh and think."

I stare at her a beat too long, thinking about how passionate she is about reaching out to the kids.

"You'll be a good chaperone next year" is all I say.

She smiles at that. "Thanks."

I lean back, satisfied. So far, I didn't say anything annoying or accidentally offensive. She's smiling and having fun. So much fuel for my Delia Daydreams later.

"Can I have everybody's attention, please?" Two church members who are just a year or two older than us, a guy named Joshua and a girl named Jessica, stand at the front of the room on a mini stage. They both have microphones in their hands and shirts on that say, "The Rockin' Lock-In!" The room quiets down after a few kids shush each other.

"Welcome to this year's lock-in . . . and this year, you guessed it, we're rockin'! Rockin' for the Lord!" Joshua and Jessica laugh really hard at this joke, and I almost dissolve from the secondhand embarrassment.

"We have a bunch of cool things planned for you guys tonight, some things we've never done before. So get ready to get your praise, worship, and fellowship on. But first, let's get our *prayer* on, and bless the food that the good people at Tony's Pizza Parlor have prepared for us."

Jessica leads us in prayer, asking God to bless both the food and the night. Although I've been to so many of these things, I let myself get just a little excited. I mean, Dillie said we'd be sticking together. Who knows what else the night would bring?

After prayer, Jessica, Joshua, Samantha, Mr. Wilson, and Mrs. Rochester place boxes of pizza at the front of the room and tell us to help ourselves. Dillie and I file in line, with both of us getting ample slices of pepperoni.

"I wish they had chicken and banana peppers." She blows on her pizza and we go back to her seat.

"Yeah, I know that's your favorite," I say, and I stop for a second and resist the urge to smack myself in the forehead. *Why* would I say that?

She blows on her pizza again and looks up at me with a smirk. "How did you know that?"

Uh-oh. I heard it on her LiveClip a couple days ago, but she doesn't know that. Should I tell her? "Uh—" I take a bite out of my pizza to stall, and it instantly feels like my mouth is on fire. This pizza is *hot.* No wonder Dillie kept blowing on it. I try to chew through it but I don't want to lose any taste buds. I don't want to spit it out either because that's gross. I suck in air to cool my mouth down.

Way to go, Darren. A definite sign not to say anything else.

Dillie chuckles a little while I take my glass of punch and cool what feels like smoke in my mouth.

"Are you all right?" she asks.

I nod, running my tongue along the roof of my mouth to see if it's still intact. "Yeah. Just hungry, I guess."

I blow on my pizza a few times before I trust myself to take another bite. We eat in silence for a while.

We make eye contact and I smile at her, hoping there's no pizza stuck in my teeth.

She smiles back, chuckling a little. She probably thinks I'm extremely goofy, and not like that Disney movie with the amazing soundtrack that came out in the nineties. She rolls her eyes. I'm wondering if it's because there *is* something in my teeth, when a miniature version of Dillie sits down right beside me.

"What do you want, Tara?" Dillie asks. "Darren, this is my sister, Tara."

Tara looks up at me and waves, then puts her face in her hands and sighs dramatically.

"I'm going to the bathroom when the choir performs," she says.

Dillie shakes her head. "Why? Nobody told you to quit children's choir just because you didn't like the early morning practices."

"That's not why I quit," she says defensively.

"You sing?" I ask her. I almost say, You sing, too? But I stop myself.

"Yes, I can sing." I note that she says this matter-of-factly, not like she's bragging or trying to convince herself, but the same way someone would say, "My shirt is green." I can tell she has the same confidence as her sister. "But I'm kind of shy about it."

That add-on is something I would say, to make it seem like I wasn't bragging on myself.

"No you aren't," Dillie says. "You sing around the house all the time."

"Yes I am. And it's different when you're singing on*stage*."

"But it's not like we can hear you individually. You're a part of a choir!"

"You heard me when I had that solo and my voice cracked and people laughed at me!"

Ah, there it is, I think to myself.

Dillie rolls her eyes. "That was one time, like six months ago. Did you think you were never going to mess up? People probably forgot about it by now anyway."

"That's easy for *you* to say. You can just edit out the parts when you mess up on your show."

Dillie glares at her sister, then shrugs. "Touché."

"I quit choir, too," I blurt out.

Tara turns to look at me. "Why?"

"I—"

I can't believe I just said that, but I didn't want Tara to feel alone. And, for a second, it was nice not to feel so alone myself.

Dillie looks up at me from the punch she's drinking.

Should I tell them? I decide against it. "I don't know, really."

Tara nods. "I get it."

"But you know . . ." I think carefully. I wouldn't want Tara to be stuck in this weird mystery singer situation I'm stuck in one day. "It's okay if you messed up once. If you love something, you should stick to it."

It's not lost on me that I'm giving advice I'm not taking. But her situation is different, less humiliating.

Kind of.

She nods and grins, a toothy one identical to Dillie's. "Thanks. I'll think about it."

Dillie sucks her teeth. "I literally tell you that all of the time."

"Well, it's different coming from a fellow singer. Plus, you're my sister and you think you know everything anyway. Bye!" She hops up and goes back to the table with her friends.

"Sisters," she says, shaking her head playfully.

"Tell me about it."

"Are you and Zoe close?"

I nod. "Pretty close. Of course we butt heads, though. She used to boss me around a lot when we were younger." I don't add that she still tries.

"Tara always says I'm bossy." Dillie sighs. "But she doesn't realize that I'm just trying to help her. I mean, she's so smart and an amazing singer. But she gives up so easily."

"Maybe you should back off a bit," I muse out loud, thinking of my own experiences with people telling me how and when to sing, then instantly regret it when Dillie's eyes narrow.

"What?" she says, her head snapping toward me.

"Oh—no, I mean . . . Zoe was always well-meaning but she was so pushy it felt a little suffocating sometimes. Maybe just . . . give her space to figure it out?"

"You don't even know Tara," she says, her eyes still narrowed but with a hint of a smile at least.

"No, but I know how it is to have a bossy older sister."

What am I *saying*?

"So, do you agree that I'm bossy?" Dillie asks.

I don't think she's bossy, but Tara does. That's all I mean.

I shrug. "Tara said it, not me."

I'm worried that I came off as too nonchalant, but Dillie laughs at that, luckily, and I take a bite out of my pizza, which is finally at an acceptable temperature to eat.

I lean back, chewing. *Relax*, I tell myself. I clearly need to keep the conversation away from singing. It's too personal, making me say opinions I haven't had the chance to think through. Plus, I don't need to give anyone clues that I'm the mystery singer.

As if on cue, Jessica and Joshua go back to the front of the room, and everyone quiets down.

"Okay, everyone! We hope that you're enjoying your meal. You can keep eating, but we're about to get our worship on as the youth choir gets rockin'. We ask that if you want another slice, you do so now so you won't block the view of the experience!" Joshua says.

"However, we won't fault you for getting up off your feet and moving to the beat," Jessica adds, and the two of them do a small hip bump.

"Can they be any more corny?" Dillie asks, and I laugh.

"I'm going to get some more pizza. Do you want anything?"

Her eyes brighten. "Ooh, yes! More pizza, please!"

I make my way back to the food table and grab a couple of slices of pizza. I watch the choir set up on the stage, and I feel Tara's sentiments exactly. Maybe I should go hide in the bathroom, too.

I sit down just as the lights dim and pass Dillie her plate.

A familiar gospel song blares over the speakers, and the youth choir starts dancing, each doing something different, but moving to the same beat.

They sound amazing. Even the kids who thought they were too cool to be here eventually ice off and start clapping their hands. I see Tara watching the choir with a stoic face, although she's nodding along to the beat.

They transition immediately to another song I know well. A guy who I recognize as a freshman at my school starts singing the solo to lead the choir.

My solo. Well, it used to be my solo, a long time ago. I look around at the crowd and people hoot and holler. I hear the familiar calls of "Take your time!" and "You better sing!"

"He sounds okay," Dillie says. "Just a little off-key, though. Right?"

I don't say anything as I work on my pizza. I feel a twinge of . . . something. Dillie just mentioned that he was a little off-key. Isn't that one of the reasons I don't want to sing anyway? The unwanted opinions?

I think about what I told Tara. Does that same thing apply to me?

The guy onstage finishes the solo and the audience claps as the choir sings the rest of the song.

After a few more songs and a slightly overfull belly from dinner, we see Jessica and Joshua go to the front of the room yet again.

"Didn't they sound amazing?" Jessica asks. Everyone cheers in response, except for Tara, I notice.

"I hope you all have digested that pizza, because it's time for all of us to get on our feet in the name of the Lord," Joshua says. "It's time for the Praise Fest!"

The lights dim again, replaced with something similar to strobe lights. Gospel music blares from the speakers again, and Jessica and Joshua start jumping up and down and clapping. Soon, as Joshua suggested, everyone is on their feet, including Dillie and me.

At first I feel a little corny. But it's dark, the music's good, and it's actually . . . fun. We've never done a Praise Fest like this before. Usually, the youth choir sings throughout the night and we watch them. This time, though, they're on the floor, jumping around and holding their hands to the sky just like the rest of us.

A few songs later, I look over at Dillie. She's sweating, curls coming out of her bun, and she's yelling the words.

Lord! You are so good. I'm so thankful for your grace!

This is one of my favorite worship songs, so I yell the words, too. Everyone is, so no one will be able to pick out my voice in the crowd. There are no pretenses, no mystery singing . . . just doing what I love . . . a few feet away from my crush.

After a few more slower worship songs, where people were crying and swaying and holding themselves, everyone sits down, slightly exhausted from all the emotion. I look up at Dillie and am surprised to find she's already staring at me, with bright eyes and flushed cheeks.

"That was . . . fun!" she says, breathing a little heavy.

"I know, right? Who would've thought?"

"I told you this time could be different."

I look at her and smile, genuinely content. She was right. I've never been so happy to be wrong.

Jessica and Joshua come to the front of the stage once again, sweating just like the rest of us.

"I hope you're not too tired of singing, because we have one more vocal-related treat for you," Jessica announces.

Dillie and I look at each other. Was Mary Mary coming to sing to us, too?

"It's almost midnight, so we'll be going right into the midnight social," Joshua says. "We have a few treats up here for you on the food table."

I look up at the table and sure enough, the empty pizza boxes have been cleared out and my dad's desserts, along with what looks like an ice cream bar, have replaced them.

"But we also have . . ." Jessica looks at Joshua and I can tell they're silently counting to three to say the next words at the same time.

"A karaoke machine!"

My stomach flips, then drops as everyone around me claps. For a second, I get excited. Karaoke is supposed to be fun; no one cares if you mess up or not. But then I realize . . . I can't sing karaoke. Unless I want Dillie to know I'm the mystery singer.

I could tell her tonight.

Should I?

Dillie glances at her sister and Tara turns around from the table she's sitting at, seemingly feeling her sister's eyes drilling into the back of her head.

"We've loaded up a bunch of great worship songs that you can sing alone or in a group," Joshua says. "To break the ice, we'll start!"

Joshua and Jessica walk over to the karaoke machine and take a few minutes to find a song. They don't really sing it, they mostly talk through it, but the coordinated yet uncoordinated choreography they came up with to go with it is enough to make me want to go home.

"They are really doing the most," Dillie says, with a headshake and a chuckle.

"I guess this is their idea of Rockin' with the Lord," I say to myself, but I must've been louder than I thought, because Dillie laughs so hard, she snorts.

A few middle schoolers get up and do some songs in groups. They giggle through them, and we clap and laugh with them after each performance. Then, I hear someone say, "My turn."

I look up and realize Tara isn't in her seat anymore, but at the front of the room, searching for a song on the karaoke machine.

"It looks like your sister is about to start singing again," I point out. Dillie gasps and takes out her phone to record it.

She chooses a Tamela Mann song, which I thought was ambitious for a middle schooler, but clearly I was wrong. Tara can't just sing—she can *sang*. Everyone is on their feet by the end of the performance, cheering her on. I can't believe she was never going to sing again just because her voice cracked one Sunday morning. That so many people would miss out on *that* voice.

I wonder if anyone has ever thought that about me. Probably not. Mr. Wilson didn't even realize I quit the youth choir.

After her performance, Tara bypasses her table and comes to sit down beside us. "How did I do?" she asks.

"You were incredible," I say. "I haven't heard someone sing that well in a long time."

"Thanks!" She beams. "It felt really good to sing such a hard song and do it right."

"I told you, little sis. You're amazing. I bet you felt good being onstage again too, huh?"

"I did . . ." she trails off and looks at me. "Are you going to sing? This could be the ex-choir kids' section of the program."

I look at the karaoke machine and hesitate. I think about Mr. Wilson asking me if I was singing tonight. Even though I'm always Wyatt's son or Zoe's brother to him, for those few seconds, I was recognized for my own thing.

If I sing, it'll automatically give away that I'm the mystery singer. But maybe that wouldn't be so bad.

"I—"

"That was fun! I hope everyone had an amazing time rockin' with us tonight! You're welcome to hang out in the game room for a little while until lights out!" Jessica yells.

Just like that, the opportunity is over. Had I been a little quicker, they probably would've let me at least finish my song before they stopped karaoke. But the steady line of kids ready to sing had dwindled and completely stopped after Tara finished. They probably thought everyone who wanted to sing did.

Maybe they were right.

Tara shrugs at me. "Oh, well. Next time."

My stomach drops as Joshua turns off the karaoke machine and takes the microphone.

"Yeah. Next time."

After playing a few games of Ping-Pong with my roommates for the night, I decide to go to the chapel to set up my sleeping area before everyone else comes in. There weren't any bedrooms in the church, so our sleeping arrangements were really just wherever our bags were placed. I'm beside two ninth graders, Malcolm and Jacob. Luckily, though, there are only two other people in the entire chapel, a girl on the far side of the room who I can't see, and Jessica, who is overseeing the chapel.

"Heading up so early?" she says as I pass her.

"Yeah. I had a long day," I reply. I didn't really, but I've been socializing a lot, and I wanted a little quiet time before I had to wake up and do it again tomorrow.

About an hour later, everyone starts filing upstairs into the chapel to prepare for lights out, including Malcolm, Jacob, Dillie, and Tara. While everyone else is mumbling and starting to look sleepy, Dillie is still as loud and energetic as ever, if not even more so. Her voice is bouncing off the stained glass and rising up to the ceiling.

She catches me looking at her, but I stare a beat too long before looking away. She crosses over a few people unrolling their sleeping bags and sighs dramatically.

"I'm not sleepy at all," she says.

"I can tell. Neither am I, though."

"Why did you come up so early? I was looking for you."

She was looking for me. I can barely hide my shock. My . . . excitement.

"I just needed some quiet time. You know, time to think."

"Ah" is all she says, as if she's had an epiphany about something. "What are you thinking about?"

You.

"You—you know . . . the events of the day. I just like to replay them before I go to sleep."

"Hm. Maybe I should try that."

"Did you enjoy yourself?" I ask her.

She nods, a lazy smile on her face. "Yeah. I really love kids. I can't wait to be a chaperone next year. It's like . . . I can help them through things I've already been through. Make it easier for someone else not to make the same mistakes I did."

When she says this, her eyes light up. It looks like she's having her own Delia Daydream.

"You sound like my grandma," I say, and then Dillie bursts out laughing.

"I didn't mean it like that," I say, shaking my head. "I mean, uh, you sound like a wise old woman."

What?

Dillie laughs so hard again, she snorts. "That's my goal in life! To be a wise old woman." Her laughter turns to quiet giggles. "Seriously, though, I love helping people. It's something I want to do on *Dillie D in the Place to Be* more."

"How will you do it?" I ask.

She sighs. "I don't know. I want to do interviews, have an advice portion and stuff like that. People are used to me talking about gossip and rambling about my day. That's always been the style. I don't know how people would like the change."

For a second, she looks troubled. I instinctively want to hug her, but I change my mind at the last minute and smooth my hands down my jacket instead.

"Are you okay?" I ask her.

She looks like she snapped out of a daydream and smiles quickly. "Yeah," she says. But I notice the smile doesn't reach her eyes. "What about you?" she asks.

"I'm okay," I tell her.

"No." She laughs, and this time it does reach her eyes. It makes me smile back. "I mean, what do you like to do? Or want to do, I guess?"

"Oh, um." I'm reminded of the conversation I had with Mrs. Thompson. "I don't know."

"Come on, it has to be *something*," she says.

What should I tell her? I can't say sing . . . she doesn't need any inkling that I'm the mystery singer. Plus, I've only just started back doing that. Kind of.

"I love doing things around church." I gesture around the chapel. Dillie stares at me, waiting for another answer. "Hanging out with my friends . . . playing basketball."

I realize this is the exact same thing I said to Mrs. Thompson.

I start to feel uncomfortable, and even a little annoyed as Dillie stares at me, clearly waiting for me to say something more interesting. I can't tell if I'm annoyed because I'm not being all the way truthful with her, or because I'm not being all the way truthful with myself.

"That's it?" she says, a little disappointed.

"What else do you want me to say?" I ask her. "Aside from making straight As, I don't really have any plans to save the world." It comes out a little harsher than I intended.

"Sheesh. Sorry," she says. "I was just saying!"

"I just—" I sigh. "I do other things but it's complicated right now, like choir is with your sister Tara. Sometimes you have to take a break from what you're passionate about to figure it out again. And that's what I'm doing."

I can't believe I just said that out loud. I'm realizing Dillie, like my mom, has a way of pulling the truth out of you.

She nods, warming back up again. "I could see that. So . . . what *is* that passion, exactly?"

I fidget a little. "Has anyone ever called you nosy?" I ask

playfully. Thankfully, she chuckles. And luckily, at that moment, Jessica yells, "Five minutes until lights out!"

Dillie groans. "I'm literally going to be staring at the ceiling for hours. I still feel like doing stuff."

A thought comes into my head: What if I ask her for her number right now? That way we could text until we fall asleep, a virtual conversation full of smiley faces and flirtation.

But then, what if she doesn't let this "What is my passion thing" go? I don't want to talk about that. I don't even understand what's going on. I get the sense that she thinks I'm boring because I'm in between having a "thing." At least this way, I can keep an air of mystery. I can't mess this up before it even starts.

I realize I'm having a Delia Daydream, right in front of Delia. She's looking at me, waiting on me to say something. I'm glad Justin isn't here to witness this. I'm just ready to imagine a better version of this conversation in my head.

"Well, let me get back to my sleeping bag before I get in 'trouble.'" She uses air quotes. "I'll see you in the morning." She walks away. I realize that she's probably walking away because I just stood there and said nothing while I was thinking. Also, because it's three minutes until lights out.

"See you." I lie back down and stare at the ceiling as Malcolm and Jacob set up their sleeping bags and talk about the JV football games from last week. From what I can gather, Malcolm is on the team.

I'm replaying the events of the day—what I could've done

better, what I could've avoided—but all in all, it was a good one. Way better than I expected, especially since I hung out with Dillie the entire night. I'm thankful I decided to come after all.

I think about how if I just could've said something to Dillie, maybe we could be texting right now. But who knows. It also could've ruined everything.

I look for a playlist on my phone, but I realize that I've already heard every worship song that I like tonight. My hand hovers over the nineties R&B playlist, but it feels so weird to play it in church. I end up on the song I made for the contest, "Dillie's Song." I listen to it for a few minutes, replaying the words. I cannot believe Jerrod sent this song in. I can't believe that I care.

And Dillie D, you're my favorite girl.

My own voice takes me out of my thoughts. It would be so easy just to tell her, right now, that I'm the mystery singer.

Singer. I think of how I felt when the youth choir was singing. How Tara looked when she sung for the first time in months. When I missed my chance at karaoke. I don't want to miss opportunities with Dillie, but was I really ready to let go of opportunities with singing, too? I needed to make up my mind, fast.

09: Dillie's Interlude I
DILLIE D IN THE PLACE TO BE TRANSCRIPT

Happy Sunday, y'all! It's yours truly, Dillie, back in the studio after a pretty eventful week and weekend.

For my fellow students, what's going on out there? Homecoming week is just around the corner for us at Jamison, and of course that means everyone is campaigning for homecoming queen and king. Is anybody out there running? I'm considering running next year . . . so keep that in mind when it's time to vote. Our school has never had a Black homecoming queen before. Can you believe that? So I'm planning to either become the first or follow a girl who does.

Homecoming means homecoming dance. Do y'all have dates yet? I don't, but I don't mind just going with my girls either. It'll be a nice break from all this SAT prep I'm doing, sheesh.

I got the creative bug and did me and my sister's hair in these cute braided-up buns. I even put a heart-shaped design in the front, which came out of nowhere. It took forever to do my sister's hair because she is so tender-headed—are any of y'all tender-headed? I'm not, so I can pull and tug at my own hair for hours—but the end result is so pretty. I'll post an eClip about it later today!

This weekend, I went to a lock-in at my church called the Rockin'

Lock-In. I know, I know, the name is kind of corny and I did feel a tad too old for it all *giggles*, but you know what? We had a really good time. Y'all know how important my faith is to me so I felt like I could, just, let it all out, you know? Special shout-out to the business that gifted me their extra-comfy lavender jumpsuit, Lavender and Lilac. Check the podcast notes for their website and a special discount code to their shop. But back to the lock-in. I got to sing a little, dance a little, eat a lot, and my little sister sung so well it almost brought me to tears. Don't tell her that of course. Speaking of music bringing me to tears . . . the mystery singer still hasn't come forward! I can't decide if I'm even more intrigued or just annoyed. Reveal yourself already!

10: Release

Another day, another intervention from Justin and Jerrod.

"Dawg," Justin starts. It's after school, the three of us at our favorite burger place, Sally's. My parents are helping out at church and Justin's parents are working late. Jerrod must have been very dedicated to this intervention because he drove across town for it.

We've just gotten our food—for me, a double cheeseburger deluxe meal with no tomatoes, fries, and a Coke.

While waiting, I casually filled Jerrod in about the lock-in. I already told Justin, and he was so fired up about me not telling Dillie about the song when I had multiple chances.

"*Dawg*," he says again, this time with his mouth full of burger. "That was the perfect opportunity! It's almost like you don't want to tell her. Would you rather just . . . date her in your head? In your Delia Daydreams?"

"Date her in your head? I don't know about that, man," Jerrod says, shaking his head and covering his burger in way too much ketchup before taking a huge bite. I glance at him. Nobody asked him. But then again, no one asked Justin either. I guess not minding their business runs in their family.

"It didn't feel right," I say, taking a sip of Coke. It really didn't. The moment needs to be perfect.

Doesn't it?

I say as much, but Justin and Jerrod shake their heads.

"It's never the exact time to do something," Jerrod says, reading my mind and taking a french fry out of the greasy cup it came in, then pointing it at me. "Think about it. When was the last time you did something worthwhile that actually started out in a perfect way?"

I have no idea. I usually play out the bad things before they happen and stop myself there. I shrug.

"Exactly," Jerrod says, seemingly satisfied with that. "You just gotta go for it and work it out as you go."

I take a big bite of my burger and roll the thought around in my head.

"All I'm saying is," Justin says, loudly, "you're doing all of this over a song. The song is just the first step. Then you have to ask her out, and then she actually has to say *yes*, then—"

"That's not helping, bruh," Jerrod says, shaking his head. "We're trying to get our friend to start with step one. Can't show him the entire hand yet."

"Well, I'm trying to tell him that he needs to hurry up and get through step one, because he's doing all of this and Dillie doesn't even know he likes her. What if she doesn't even say yes or—"

They're doing it again. Discussing me like I'm not there. I watch for a few minutes and wait and see if they ask me for input on my life.

They don't.

I finish my burger and work on the fries, still thinking about what Jerrod said, when my phone vibrates. I pick it up, expecting it to be my parents telling me they're on the way home.

It's a notification telling me that Dillie is about to do a livestream.

I click on it, then dip my fries into the ketchup, mayo, mustard mix I made.

"Hey, y'all!" she says, her big smile spreading across the screen. "I'm just procrastinating, need to be doing homework. What are y'all doing?"

Various comments come in, some saying they're procrastinating and not doing their homework as well, some saying they are just getting home from various practices. I type that I'm at a burger joint, then delete it, then type it again and send it.

Dillie is reading comments, her mouth moving with each one. She laughs at some, like when a girl says she's struggling to take her braids out before school tomorrow. "Oh, girl! Why didn't you wait until the weekend?" She does a fake tsk-tsk. "May the force be with you." She frowns and rolls her eyes at a random guy who comments, "Waiting on you."

"Waiting on me for what?" she says, scrolling past it.

She lands on my message. And she smiles again.

"Mm, burger joint! You know, the one I went to was trash, and the guy was racist. Tuh!"

This is my chance, the one I missed during her last livestream. I feel the urge to say, "Maybe I should take you to my favorite burger place," but I don't want to say this over livestream. It's not right.

"You should tell her you'll bring her here sometime!" Justin echoes my thoughts, Jerrod nodding. I realize they're watching me watch the LiveClip.

"It's not—" I say, then suck my teeth when Jerrod starts shaking his head at me.

"That's not even step one. It's step zero, or negative one. You can do this."

"But you better hurry up," Justin says. "The comments are going fast."

It's true. I think about it, take a deep breath, and dump a whole bunch of fries into my mouth. This is small. And not harmful. I could do this.

I type, "Maybe I should take you sometime." And delete it. Too vague. No call to action.

I try, "I'll take you one day."

One day? Again, too vague.

I type, "Next time you're craving a burger, I can take you."

It gives a time (whenever she's craving a burger again), shows effort (I'll take her, not meet her there), and gives her the space to decline ("I can take you, but I don't have to, if you don't want").

But then I picture her looking at the message and I imagine her disgust, or worse, smiling politely and declining in front of everyone. And once she declines, that's it. I'd have to move on.

No. It has to be perfect.

Justin and Jerrod are looking at their phones until Justin realizes that I did not send the message.

"What are you waiting on?" Justin asks.

I say nothing, continue eating my fries. Instead, I type, "I know a better spot." And after agonizing over it for thirty seconds, I click send. Nice and safe.

Dillie continues reading comments and stumbles upon mine again. She laughs this time.

"I'm gonna hold you to that, Darren," she says. "I'm sure it won't be long before I'm craving a double cheeseburger deluxe with no tomatoes."

"She's gonna hold you to it," Jerrod says.

"I'm watching, just like you are," I say, giving him a raised eyebrow.

He missed it, though, the part where she mentioned the same meal I'm eating now.

"Haha, I'm actually eating that same thing right now," I type and send without thinking.

She goes directly to my comment. "Nuh-uh! I don't believe you. Bring your receipt to school tomorrow."

I type back, "Will do," when my phone buzzes again.

Justin scoffs. "Way to *not* be romantic, Darren. Pretty soon you're just going to be her local food critic."

Oh no. Is he right?

"Don't listen to Justin. I consider it a step in the right direction, dawg," Jerrod says, holding up his soda in tribute.

But now I'm not so sure. Maybe I shouldn't have said *anything*.

My phone buzzes again: my parents texting me and telling me they're on the way home.

I text my mom back and return to Dillie's LiveClip.

Someone has asked her if she's found out who the mystery singer is.

She sighs, sets her cheeks in her hands. "Not yet," she says. "But I'm starting to get restless. If it was just a little theme song, I'd be over it by now. But they said all those things about me, you know? I wanna know who feels this way about me."

Justin and Jerrod look up at me slowly, the way a TV character looks at a camera when he breaks the fourth wall in a show.

"Nope," I say, without even looking at them. I stuff the rest of the french fries in my mouth. "Are y'all ready?"

They nod and we get up, gather our trash, leave a tip, and head outside.

"Well, what are y'all about to do?" Justin asks. "My parents aren't home yet, so I'm about to see if Tiffany wants to come over . . ." He trails off.

"I need to head back to my side of town. Oh, guess what?" Jerrod says, a big grin spreading across his face, flashing his bottom grill in the sun.

"What's up?" I ask.

"Destiny said she wants to talk things over when she gets out of cheerleading practice. I'm about to get my girl back. Hopefully."

"Good luck," I say, while Justin daps him up.

"Yeah, should I get some flowers or something?"

"See what she wants first," Justin says. "When Tiff says she wants to talk, it usually leads to us being Off Again."

"Dang, Justin, way to be supportive," I say.

Justin holds up his hands. "I just want him to be prepared!"

"I don't care, I at least gotta try." Jerrod stares off into space for a while, then snaps his finger. "I know what I'll get. Aye, I'll holla at y'all later."

I dap up Jerrod before he jogs to his car, but right before, he stops with his leg in midair. He sets it down slowly and turns around, like he's listening to something.

I hear it, too. I thought it was somewhere in the back of my head, but the sound is getting louder and louder.

"Do y'all hear that?" Jerrod asks.

It's real.

Louder and clearer we hear it. First the bassline, then the voice.

My voice.

We watch as a car drives by, windows down, volume up, as my song blares from the speakers.

"Stop whatever you're doing, stop whatever you're doing . . ."

By the time the car drives directly past us, the bass is so loud we can't even hear my voice anymore. But the car doesn't stop, the driver doesn't recognize us as the creators. The car drives away.

Justin, Jerrod, and I all look at each other in confusion.

Were they playing my song?

11: Remix

My song is blowing up.

Apparently, a kid at Dillie's old school who listens to the show heard the song, loved it, and used it as background music for the homecoming dance-posal he made for his girlfriend.

When he posted the dance-posal on social media, a bunch of people asked who was singing the song he played and where they could download it.

He told them that he didn't know, that it was a mystery, and that he just liked it so much, he decided to use the audio from Dillie's podcast and use it as background music.

From there, other people started doing the same thing.

People have been using it as background music for videos of their outfits, their faces, their food. One girl used it in a dedication post to her boyfriend.

The song was everywhere, overnight, and nobody knew who was behind it. Nobody knew that voice was mine.

And everybody loves it.

It's almost enough to make me want to start singing again,

to erase the sting of what happened *that* night. Finally, people understand me and what I want to do with my music.

I smile when I see a Clip comment saying that the singer is great. That they can feel the passion in my words.

I'm in my one-person play without having to take directions or read the reviews. And from the ones I did read, people really seem to like my voice and the track.

It should feel better than this. Somehow, it's not playing out as well as I thought it would in my head.

But why?

Is it because I didn't write the script?

"You ready, D?" Jerrod says.

I nod, even though I'm not. The uncool, too-fast nod you give when you're trying to convince the person you're okay so they can look away, and let you *not* be okay in peace.

What am I doing?

I take a deep breath. I decide that maybe the only way to feel better about this mystery singer mess is to finish my song—if it's going to be out there, it at least needs to be completed. If this song wins the contest, maybe I'll actually come forward.

I adjust my headphones, look down at the microphone in front of me, the scribbled lyrics on the unfolded piece of paper from the yellow legal pad. I see Justin, Jerrod, and the engineer, Jack, looking at me through the glass window.

Singing in the car on the way to school is different. I'm all by myself. I can play with new notes that have never seen the light of day. Adding the much-needed harmony to a group of people singing "Happy Birthday" is also different. People will look your way for a few seconds, say something like, "Wow, okay, Darren!" and then go on about their business.

Today, the attention is on me, my voice. All of it.

"All right. Let's start."

The track plays a little bit before I come in with my lyrics. There's no chorus, only the one verse since it's just a theme song for Dillie.

> *Stop whatever you're doing*
> *Stop whatever you're doing*
> Dillie D in the Place to Be, *you are the girl I'm pursuing*
> *In love with the fragrance you're using*
> *No time for fakes I'm assuming*
> *I'm a real one that can match your fly*
> *Often mistaken for a shy guy*
> *But I just*
> *don't like to waste my*
> *time*
> *But I would spend my time with you because*
> *You are so fine*
> *Brown skin*
> *Brown hair*
> *Brown eyes*

Your ambition and drive
Your hips and thighs
I'm mesmerized
But I want to make this dream a reality
Together just you and me, we
Complement each other so nicely
You're a star and I'm low-key
Power couple in the making
The world is ours for the taking
You're the one I want to be dating
I've said my part, I'll let you do the rest
This is my shot, I've tried my best
Let me take you out, let me be your man
Delia Dawson, won't you say yes?

I sing, the notes flowing out mostly effortlessly, except for a few notes that I know I can do better by. Maybe it *is* time for me to get out of my comfort zone. This feeling is both familiar and new. I guess it's worth a try.

This takes me back to a time when I sung every Sunday at church. Little quiet Darren, with the big voice for the Lord on Sundays. I remember picking up the too-heavy microphone, some of the elders in the front with their big church hats telling me to "Take your time, baby!" as I sung a version of "Amazing Grace." The congregation would stand up and clap every Sunday. It was a happy place and time.

Church is still a happy place for me, don't get me wrong. My parents started going after they got married. They tried a handful until they found one that made them feel right at home. I've grown up there, in the same pew we've been sitting in for as long as I can remember. We do a lot for each other, for the community, for God.

But the more I sang, the more people wanted me to sing, not for myself, not for God, but for *them*. People started asking me to sing on the spot, anywhere and everywhere. Then, asking turned into suggestions:

"Why don't you sing it this way?"

"What are you doing? Shouldn't you be practicing your solo?"

"Can I watch you practice?"

Then, suggestions became telling:

"You're free next Saturday, right? Because I've booked you to sing at Aunt Brenda's surprise birthday party."

"You know that new show where they try to find the next big thing? I sent in a submission for you—a recording of you singing last Sunday."

"You may need to be on vocal rest. I noticed you didn't go for the note like you usually do. You sounded kind of hoarse, too."

The last one was a random Clip Message I got from a member of the church, an older person who is also part of the choir. I've never really done well with criticism, but that message got to me. I guess because she didn't know the real story: that I was getting over a cold but still wanted to sing my solo. I thought that I did fairly well for someone with a scratchy throat.

After that, I gradually faded myself out from the church choir and decided to join the school chorus instead. It was a totally different style of singing, almost a challenge to the riffs and runs I was used to, but where in church I really relied on singing from the heart, school chorus helped me learn technique. I even became the lead of my section. Then people started to notice and give more opinions that no one asked for. I sounded great *here*, but not so great *there*. I was too modest to some people (Why don't you sing MORE?!) and too arrogant for others (Why don't you sing LESS?!). It was annoying.

Somewhere along the way, singing became about everyone else, and I just stopped. I thought I could sing in my little bubble, though, or do my own thing, and everything would be fine.

Then the horrid open mic night happened, and I made everything worse.

But as Mom says, God works in strange ways, so here I am, in a stuffy recording studio, singing a theme song for a podcast hosted by the girl of my dreams, anonymously.

I end the song on a note that I'm not too sure about, and I look up to find Justin, Jerrod, and Jack gaping at me.

"I know the ending was a little rough, but—"

"Bruh, you can really sing," Jerrod says. "I thought maybe that studio session was just a fluke, but you seriously—"

"I'm okay," I say, shifting under the attention.

Jerrod's face looks blank, but you can tell there are a million thoughts running through his head. He finally says, "Do you know how much money you could make singing hooks on rap songs? Similar to what Nate Dogg did?"

"I've never thought about it," I say, which is true.

"You need to start a singing channel," Justin says. "You could get a record deal, easily! Just upload a few times a week—"

"There's an audition coming up for *An American Vocalist* around here next month," says Jack. "My cousin works at the venue. I can see about getting you in. . . ."

"I don't know, man, I still like the other track better," Justin says. "That'll be something they'll play in all of the clubs and parties. This one has more a slow-dance feel."

"I personally think they're both good, I guess because I made them," Jerrod says. "But I agree. Are you sure you don't want to rerecord the whole song again on the faster track?"

It was happening again. Already.

"No," I say, a little forcefully. Jack, Jerrod, and Justin all look at me, surprised. I come out of the booth.

"This song . . . this song has to be perfect." I take a deep breath. "Especially in case it does win and I do decide to come forward. Because I don't want a repeat of what happened last time."

The three of them are still staring at me.

"What are you talking about?" Justin says.

I sigh. "The open mic night?"

Justin furrows his brow and lets out a loud guffaw. "Yo, you gotta be kidding. You weren't even serious, and nobody will remember that!"

"What is open mic night?" Jerrod asks.

I really don't want to relive the night, but it's the only way they'll understand how important this song is for me.

One day, Justin, Tiffany, and I went out to see Tiffany's sister do spoken word at one of the local colleges. Don't ask me how I ended up being the third wheel at something like this, because I don't even know.

Anyway, Tiffany's sister performs her poem and does a great job, and the host decides to open up the floor for open mic night. This was around the time when I was feeling so much pressure from school chorus, and I had spent the past few nights writing an original song. Nobody knew me at this college, so I felt like everything would be great.

Except—it wasn't. I was too in my head, too worried about messing up. The song was supposed to be about letting go and doing things my way but I couldn't even do it. Maybe I sounded technically okay, but I knew I didn't seem or sound very confident. Confidence is key in a situation like that. Looking back on it, I was probably boring, too.

"*Boo!*" someone in the very back of the crowd yelled. In Justin and Tiffany's defense, they did try to shut the person up, but when one person boos . . .

"*Womp womp!*" The rest of the crowd started waving their hands in the air, from side to side in the motion reminiscent of

It's Showtime at the Apollo, where the crowd is eager to get the performer off the stage.

I tried to sing over the jeers but decided to sit down just in case Sandman Sims was ready to shoo me off the stage in shame.

"That was great!" Justin laughed, but he didn't actually mean great, he meant, "I can't believe you went up there and embarrassed yourself."

"I thought you sounded okay," Tiffany said. "This is just . . . a really serious, artsy crowd. They only like serious singers."

Serious singers. If I wasn't a serious singer, then what kind of singer was I?

Not one at all.

To make matters worse, I searched the school on eClips, and some people had taken video of my performance and posted it to their pages.

"Who is this guy? Snooooze," I remember one post saying.

"Where was the passion? He sung like he was reading a script."

That one hurt.

And the one that hurt the most: "He was incredibly flat."

I had played it safe and I didn't want to risk my voice cracking. But I guess it doesn't matter.

"Oh . . . well, my bad, man. I didn't think you were actually *serious* up there," Justin says as my flashback gives way to the present. "I mean . . . you weren't even singing like you were serious. You were going through the motions, like 'Let me get up here and sing so I can say I did.' Like you were dared to or something."

I frown at Justin and he shrugs.

"That's tough, man, but sometimes we artists have bad nights," Jerrod chimes in. "You'll bounce back, especially with this song."

"I just want to finish this song and get it over with," I say. "Let's focus on that for now."

They quiet down momentarily as we go through the song and rerecord certain lines and add harmonies.

"Your doubles . . . are amazing," Jack says as he mixes my voice, with my voice. "You're, like, a harmony king."

"I appreciate it" is all I say. But the compliment feels good. Jack doesn't know me from a can of paint. He doesn't have a reason to lie, he gets paid either way. And it feels better because, as bizarre as this situation is, I still care about how I sound, and I worked hard to sound good.

Soon, we're finished, the recording is mastered, and Jerrod is prepping to send the file from the same email address he sent my unapproved recording.

"So what's your stage name?" Jerrod asks.

"I don't have one," I reply. "Send it anonymously."

"Again?" Jerrod, Justin, and Jack all say at the same time.

"Yeah. There's no point in revealing that I'm the one who wrote the song yet. If I win . . . we'll . . . cross that bridge when we get to it."

"Why are you prolonging this?" Justin says, an edge of irritability to his voice. "The minute you tell Dillie that this is your song, you'll know if she's interested in you or not *and* everyone will know you can sing!"

"That's exactly why I'm prolonging it!"

"But *why*—" Justin starts again.

"Chill, cousin. Us artists have special demands like this. Our thought processes are very unique," Jerrod says. "Fine. We won't say anything now. But of course, if you win, you'll have to. And the way this song is literally everywhere right now? I have no doubt it'll happen." He continues typing on his laptop and looks back up a few minutes later.

"Sent."

Justin accepts Jerrod's reasoning, even though I catch him looking at me incredulously out of the corner of my eye. But what Jerrod said is right. We don't have to say anything now, but we obviously would if we win.

Even though winning the contest has benefits that I could only dream of, and I mean literal Delia Daydreams, the prospect of telling Dillie how I feel while doing something I really love? The prospect of winning in real life? It's a little scary, I'm not gonna lie.

12: Dillie's Interlude II
DILLIE D IN THE PLACE TO BE TRANSCRIPT

*My friends and I were talking about this last night, so I had to bring it
to the podcast! Do you prefer to shower at night or in the morning?*

*I gotta say, I love a morning shower. If I'm doing a wash-and-go style
on my hair that day, I can let it dry on my way to school . . . and maybe
it'll be dry by lunchtime. It helps wake me up, too. I'm not really a morning
person. Plus, after I finish doing podcast stuff and all of my homework?
I literally could just fall asleep on my bed. Not to mention my little sister
takes her shower at night and uses up all of the hot water. Now if I decide
to take a bath and read, paint my nails, or wear a face mask at the end
of the day . . . that's a different story! So, bubble baths at night, showers
in the morning. What do y'all think?*

*Did anyone listen to the new Louis Dot album yet? How do y'all feel
about it? I know I probably sound like a broken record at this point, but
I absolutely loved it! The way he sings, you can feel the emotion in each
and every word! I swear, I almost cried when I heard "I Wish You Loved
Me, Too." It's a voice I can get lost in. Let me know what you think in
my Clip comments!*

*Now, the mystery singer on the other hand . . . he sent in a full version
of the original song. I replay that version over and over again. I know some*

of you are thinking, "How self-centered is that?!" But . . . not only are the lyrics so sweet, but his voice is, too. That is another voice I could get lost in. Mystery singer, whoever you are, you have a huge gift. A way with words and a voice to match. I can't wait to find out who you are! I'll play it for y'all. Let me know what you think!

13: Cover Artist

Writing, recording, and sending in the new version of the song felt like a weight lifted off my shoulders. It felt completely true to the music I like to make. Dillie said on her podcast that she loves it. It made me happy.

The next morning on the way to school, when I park and turn off the car, I hear the old, muffled version of the song blaring from somewhere in the parking lot. I wonder if people will still like the new version, or if they'll be tired of it from hearing the old version too much.

"You hear that?" Justin says, jogging toward me as we walk through the science atrium, the song slowly fading away. "The song is everywhere now. You're an overnight celebrity, man!"

"Shhh," I say, motioning with my hand for him to keep it down, although no one looks our way.

"What—don't tell me you still don't want people to know. Darren, you could be getting a date *and* a record deal!"

I walk to my locker, lost in thought. The idea of everybody liking something I did, without me ever having to hear their opinions about what I should do next, was—

"Confusing," Justin says, shaking his head. "You confuse me, man! Two things you really want, right in front of you, and you're about to blow it because you don't want to take credit."

"I don't want a record deal" is all I say. At least, I think I don't.

"Real life is happening while you're in your head, you know. This song is not gonna be hot forever."

I slow at that. It was everywhere now, but even as soon as next week, the song could be old. It is only for Dillie—who would probably be getting tired of this soon, too. Whatever *this* was.

"That's true." At least I can admit that.

"I know you think I'm hounding you," Justin says, as we continue to navigate the crowded hallway.

"Yup," I say. I could admit that, too.

"But I'm not! Do you think I would care if the song wasn't good? Shoot, if that was the case, I'd be on the phone with Jerrod telling him to pursue rap right now! I just don't want to see you waste your talent, something you clearly want to pursue, even if you pretend you're too cool to care."

I scrunch up my face, the way I do when we have an argument on the best rappers of all time and Justin says whatever new, hot rapper is out holds the title.

"I'm not trying to be too cool—" I start.

"You don't have to admit it to me. Just to yourself." The conversation is over now (as if I'd ever wanted it to start) because Tiffany walks over.

"Hey, Darren." She waves. I throw up two fingers in response.

Tiffany is a cool enough girl, and I know that somewhere in Justin's heart, he loves her. But their relationship is so confusing, and Tiffany doesn't speak to me at all when she and Justin are Off Again. So, we went from calling each other "Bro!" or "Sis!" to just keeping it nice and cordial to make things less awkward.

But this time, as I try to walk past her to my own locker, she keeps the conversation going. "Have you heard the new song?" Her head whips around to me.

"I—" I glance at Justin, who shrugs and mouths, "I didn't tell her!" behind her back.

"Uh, talking about the one with Dillie's name in it?" I ask.

She nods excitedly. "Yeah! Isn't it cool?"

I shrug a little. "Yeah, it's pretty nice."

"It's so cool *and* romantic"—she throws this word in Justin's direction—"that someone would make a song about being a secret admirer. I wonder who it is." She looks dreamy. "He can really sing, too."

I'm not convinced that Justin didn't have anything to do with the conversation.

"Do you know who it is?" I ask her, glancing at Justin.

She taps a purple, manicured nail to her chin for a second. "A lot of people think it's Miles."

The air leaves my lungs and my stomach flips.

"Miles?"

Miles?

She nods excitedly. "Yup! He's been putting all these little hints on social media. He hasn't confirmed it yet, though, and he hasn't responded to anyone who's asked him. I don't know, maybe he's planning this big thing. I mean, he's cute but"—she scrunches up her nose and lowers her voice—"honestly, Dillie can do *way* better."

With that, she turns and gives Justin a hug and a kiss and I take that as my cue to continue to walk to my locker.

I can't believe people think Miles is the singer. And why is he letting people think he is?

I'm pulled out of my thoughts by the smiling face I see by my locker. For a second, I'm not sure if my thoughts are taking over my real life—that Dillie's grin isn't getting bigger, her eyes aren't gleaming playfully—as I walk closer.

"What's up?" I ask her, but I know it comes out a little faster than I intended to.

"Hey, Darren!" she says. She leans against my locker, comfortably, as if she always does this.

"Do you remember when I said Andy's Burger Joint was racist?" she says. The senior at his locker behind her looks up uncomfortably and walks away. Maybe he likes Andy, or maybe he is also racist.

"Yeah . . ." I say, as the guy passes both of us. Dillie glances at him and keeps talking.

"Well, that sucks because I really want a burger today. And then I remembered that you said you knew of a better spot. Are you in the mood to join me?"

I stare at Dillie, trying to make sense of what's going on. Does she want to go to Sally's? With me? What if I suggest it and she laughs in my face and walks away?

Or is this the perfect moment I've been waiting for? How can it be, if—

Her smile falters a bit. "I mean, unless you don't—"

"*NO!*" I yell, and she flinches. Of all the times Dad's yelling gene could come out, it has to be right now? "Sorry, I didn't mean—"

"No, it's cool, I—"

"No, no, Dillie, I mean it's great. Do you want to go at lunch? Let's go at lunch. Let's meet in the parking lot. I'll drive." This all comes out in one breath.

"Well, okay. See you then!" She walks away and I'm left standing there in disbelief.

Dillie and I are going on a date.

14: Dreamgirl

There's a song on one of my parents' playlists, "I'm Dreamin'" by a man named Christopher Williams. My mom loves the words and the beat—she does the cabbage patch to it on Saturday mornings, while Dad cooks breakfast. Dad sings along, insisting his voice has the same "creamy huskiness to it" as Christopher Williams, and my mom agrees, even though the three of us know he doesn't actually think that. When I used to sing, people said I got my voice from my great-grandfather, Jerome. He sang loud and powerfully every Sunday in church until he passed away at 102.

My parents call "I'm Dreamin'" my theme song. My dad says it should be playing every time I walk into a room. *"Don't wake me, I'm dreamin'"* because I like whatever I'm dreaming about more than what's happening around me. Usually, that is really the case. I can have exactly what I want, without the potential bad stuff or criticism.

Now, though, as I'm on the way to Sally's with Dillie riding in the passenger seat, the windows down and her light brown afro blowing all over her face, I'm suddenly not so sure that anything I could've dreamed would be better than this. It makes me wonder what other surprises are waiting for me outside my head.

When I pictured this moment in my head, I thought I'd have on my favorite pair of Jordan sneakers, the 13s, but instead I'm wearing the 4s. I pictured having a fresh haircut, but it's the middle of the week and I get my hair cut on Fridays. I pictured my car being immaculately clean, but the outside is dusty, and Dillie doesn't know there is a lone, stale bag of potato chips under her seat.

But if I had to choose between the perfect version of this moment in my head and the one where Dillie pulled down the visor and a bunch of random papers flew out and into her lap, it'd be this one.

"I'm telling you, no other burger will compare," I say, as we turn out of the school parking lot for lunch. I don't even know what I'm saying. I haven't had time to mentally prepare a script of funny and charming things to say. This is improv, and I have to roll with it.

"I hope you're sure," she says, "I am so hungry, and I'm tired of having bad burgers by nice cooks or okay burgers by racist cooks."

"You don't have to worry," I say, stopping at the red light. "Sally loves everyone. She's always providing free food at the end of protests and stuff."

"A burger with a purpose." Dillie smiles. "I like that."

Dillie shuffles the envelopes that fell into her lap and starts to put them back in the visor clip.

"Sorry about that," I say. "That's just my go-to spot to put paper and stuff."

"I get it. Mine is my purse." She opens the visor and stops. "This is an old church program. You had a solo that day," she says, scanning it. She looks at me. I catch her glance before the light turns green.

"Yeah," I say.

"Speaking of church, remember the idea I told you about, helping the middle school girls? I've already talked to Jessica about maybe becoming a chaperone next year. I couldn't believe she actually listens to my show." Her cheeks turn red at this. "She said she'd love to help me put together a program for them next summer, too."

"That's a good idea. They look up to you, so no one would be better for the job."

"Thanks, Darren," she says. "I'm excited to get them ready for change and let them know that they have a girl group to support them. High school is no joke."

"I couldn't agree more."

We ride in silence for a bit, until I realize we *are* riding in silence, and I can't connect the playlist on my phone to the car when I'm driving, so I push the button for the radio. That new R&B song by Louis Dot Williams floods the airways. It's not good, but they play it all the time so I hum the music, until I realize I'm humming, then I stop.

"This is my *song!*" Dillie closes her eyes and rocks back and forth to the beat.

"Yeah . . . I—I can't believe you like this," I say. When I heard her raving about the album on her podcast, I literally sat up in bed on Sunday in disbelief. I thought Dillie loved music the way I did.

"Why not?" she asks, accusatorily.

"Um . . ."

I don't want to upset her, she clearly likes the song. But I feel the same thing happening right now that happened at the lock-in. I live in my head, but when it comes to music, something about my thoughts just wants to jump out, unchecked.

"It's—it's not good," I say.

"Not good?" she asks. "What makes it not good?"

"Well . . . I mean he's not a good singer any way you slice it," I say. "I've even heard him without the auto-tune because Justin likes him. He strains—he—he always stays on one note, he has that gravelly thing going on—"

"He sings with *emotion.*" Dillie points to the radio. "That is my favorite song right now. You know why? Because when he says, 'I wish you loved me, too,' you believe him. You really believe that there's a girl out there that doesn't love him back."

"I get that," I say. I'm still nervous about upsetting her, but I can't hold this in. Something about talking about music, about singing, excites me. For a few seconds, I can't care about what anyone thinks. I have to get this out. Which is . . . a strange feeling. "I like great lyrics as much as anybody. But I like singers who challenge themselves vocally." I sit up straighter in the driver's seat. "You know, the kind who strive for a note and then reach it, or those people whose voices are so good they were born with, like, eight octaves. I like unique voices that you're just in awe of, the ones that bring you to tears."

"Wow," Dillie says. "So, who has a voice like that?"

"Whitney Houston," I say, without hesitation.

"Well, of course Whitney Houston," Dillie says. "She was *The* Voice. Your bar is high, Darren."

It's true, it's so high I don't even think I can reach it sometimes.

"I guess so," I say. "But, I don't know, his songs are just . . . plain. I like songs with choruses and pre-choruses and bridges. His songs make me zone out." And I don't need any help doing that, I think.

"Ooh, I get it!" Dillie says, animatedly, as if she's solved a mystery. "You like songs that are, like, the total package. Like, an Usher song or something."

"Exactly!" I can't help but smile. I knew she would understand.

"But that doesn't make Louis Dot's song any less good."

"Any less good than . . . an *Usher* song?" I say, glancing at her quickly. "You can't mean that. There is no combination of any Louis Dot song that would rival even one song on Usher's *Confessions* album."

"I do," she says. "Do you know his story? He had to teach himself to produce and record his own songs with some old computer he got from a pawnshop. Sure, he's not the best vocalist or whatever, but he's doing something with what he has, and he's super relatable."

"Wow. I didn't know that." We sit quietly for a long time. Dillie has probably forgotten about our conversation when I say, "It still doesn't make me like his songs, but I have a newfound respect. Still, he could probably lose the auto-tune." I hope she realizes that I'm joking about the auto-tune part. Kind of.

"I *guess* that's fair." I can hear the smile in her voice.

I glance at her as I turn into the parking lot at Sally's. I park the car, unlock the car door, get out, and walk over to Dillie's to open hers. I don't think twice about it because it's something that me and my dad have been doing for my mom and sister since I was old enough to *open* a door.

I want Dillie to understand where I'm coming from, to not think I'm just some grumpy music critic. "Auto-tune sounds better on people who can actually sing, like T-Pain," I say as I pull the door open.

"Oh well, I guess you can't blame him for trying to do what he loves."

"True." It reminds me of the saying my mom always says: "Hard work beats talent when talent doesn't work hard."

Wait. Was she talking about me?

"Wow, a gentleman," she says as she steps out and slowly slides past me. "Hey, T-Pain is kind of like Zapp. Right?"

"Well, Zapp used a talk box, not auto-tune." I shake my head. Am I being annoying for not letting this conversation go? "I promise I'm not trying to sound like a know-it-all, I just . . . really love music."

"You know a lot about Zapp?"

"Excuse me? Zapp, who made the song ahead of their time called 'Computer Love'? Who *doesn't* know them?"

Dillie laughs as we walk toward the entrance.

"To be honest, I only know the song from middle school step team. We had a routine to it, so our captain played it ten million times, probably."

"Was that the universal step team song? Because I kind of remember my sister stepping to it back when *she* was in middle school. I guess it is a good one, though. I mean, it's so ahead of its time! They're singing about digital love in, like, 1985. It was innovative."

"It was, huh? I never thought about it like that."

I pull the door to Sally's open for the both of us. Sally walks over, a head full of short curls that are so blond they could only be rivaled by Daenerys Targaryen framing her wide, round, pink face.

"Darren!" she yells. The shop is relatively calm as the few people there sit quietly and eat their burgers and hot dogs.

"Hey, Miss Sally." I wave to her. Dillie smiles and waves, too.

"You're getting the usual?" She stands at the counter, ready to ring it up.

"Make it two of the exact same thing," I say.

Dillie scoffs, a smirk playing in the corner of her mouth.

"I'm not trying to speak for you," I say. "I just—trust me. This is your first time at Sally's, you gotta do it right."

Dillie holds up her hands in fake surrender. "Okay. I better like it though, or I'm going to roast you on the next podcast."

"But what happens *when* you like it?" I ask.

"Hmm. I haven't thought that far yet."

Sally rings us up and looks up at me, then Dillie.

"You are a beautiful girl," she says. "I don't think I've seen you in here before."

"This is Dillie—er, Delia," I say, as I hand Miss Sally my debit card.

"Dillie is fine," she says. "I go to school with Darren. This is my first time here."

"Ahh," she says. "Well, since it's your first time, like he said, you gotta do it right. If you still have room after the burgers, come back and I'll give you both a cone on the house."

"'Preciate that, Miss Sally," I say. Another nice little touch that I couldn't have created in my mind.

"Oh, don't mention it, Darren," she replies. "Y'all go on ahead and sit down and I'll bring it right to you."

So we do that. As I take the exact table that Justin, Jerrod, and I sat at just last week, I hear my song playing out of a random car.

"It's so cute in here," she says as she looks around at the red seats and white tables, the black-and-white checkered floor, the pictures on the walls of Miss Sally and various celebrities. "It's like a real diner."

"It is," I tell her. "Or, it used it to be. It runs like a regular restaurant, but Sally decided to keep the same diner vibe throughout after she remodeled in the two thousands."

"You know a lot about this place."

"I just listen," I say. "Some days, if Justin is with Tiffany and I'm craving a burger, I'll come here for lunch alone and Sally and I will talk. Or she'll do most of the talking and I listen. You hear the best stories that way."

"Hm," she says. I can't tell if she agrees with me or not, but her brown eyes are staring right into mine. "That's good logic. That's why I want to bring more guests into my studio. I spend so much time talking to myself." She laughs. "I guess I like the sound of my own voice."

"A lot of people do," I say. "I mean, that's why your podcast is so popular, right?"

"I hope so." She grins. "It's not like I'm trying to push my opinions on other people. I just need an outlet for my own thoughts, but I know my word isn't always bond. Some people don't get that, though. When I started talking about how a lot of people really don't know how to sweeten sweet tea, I got a lot of angry emails talking about how sweet tea isn't that healthy and why."

"Really? A tea rant?" I chuckle.

"And that's not even a controversial topic! We live in the south. We just want some *sweet* sweet tea. Is that too much to ask?"

"Not at all," I say. "People don't realize you have to add the sugar before the hot water and the tea to really make it sweet."

"Exactly!" she exclaims. "Someone gets it! Anyway, I'm tired of using my podcast as a diary. I'm ready to pivot to other things. I'm just nervous about it."

"Nervous?" I ask. Delia Dawson gets nervous? "I can't imagine you being nervous about anything, especially your podcast," I tell her. "I bet you could read the back of a cereal box and people would tune in."

Dillie giggles at this, a sound I want to hear forever.

"You're so funny, Darren," she says, and I can feel my cheeks split into a ridiculously huge grin. "I wish that was the case. People are used to my format, you know? I tried a few test episodes here and there, dedicated to mentorship and the stuff I want to do, and they had the lowest streams of all of my shows." She looks down and shrugs.

I feel a pang of sadness for her. "Even though the streams were low, I bet there were still a lot of people listening in," I try, fishing for a way to make her smile again. "Like, picture all of the people who listened to that show in one room. I bet the room would be full."

"Hmm. You have a point." She rests a pink painted nail on her chin. "The contest seems to be working, too. I've had twice as many listeners since I started, and so many emails surrounding the mystery singer. I mean, he is *really* popular. Out of curiosity, I asked my audience on eClips to vote for their favorite song, and his has the most by far. Maybe I should ask him to do the show with me."

"HA!" I laugh too loudly and try to cover it up with a cough.

"Are you okay?" Dillie reaches across the table and pats me on the back.

"Oh—uh, yeah. My throat is just dry. I'm just, uh, thirsty."

As if on cue, Miss Sally walks up to the two of us, holding two trays full of food.

"Two double cheeseburger deluxes, no tomatoes, double curly fries, ketchup, mustard, and mayo to mix together, two sweet teas?"

I nod as Sally puts the food down on the table for us.

"Enjoy, honey," she says to Dillie, then walks back to the counter to help the man and toddler who just walked in.

Dillie's eyes are wide as she looks at the food.

"It's a big burger, right?" I say. "You won't be hungry until dinner, or maybe even a little later."

"The tea. Is it a coincidence?" she says, narrowing her eyes a little.

"Uh—" I start to say no but tell the truth. "It's not. I heard the 'Sweet Tea Debate' episode on your podcast. Your search is over. Taste it."

"In a second," she says. I take this time to close my eyes and say a little prayer over my food. I open my eyes at the same time I realize she's opening hers.

"You say prayers before you eat, too." It's a question, but she says it like it's not.

"At first out of habit," I say, after thinking about the singsong prayers we'd sing over our food in vacation Bible school when I was little. "But now . . . man, after I worked the food drive at church last Christmas . . . I'm truly thankful for every meal."

"Yeah, I—" She pauses. "I'm thankful, too."

She takes a sip of the tea. Well, it starts like a sip, but I'm pretty sure she finishes at least half of it in one gulp.

She leans back and sighs. "Oh my *gosh*, this is the best sweet tea I've ever had!" She sits back up. "I'm so glad you have a good memory. And good taste in tea."

Me too. "I guess something came from that 'Sweet Tea Debate' after all."

"Yeah. I agree." I don't know if I'm imagining it, but I think her eyes sparkle a little bit.

"Don't tell my dad, but I think Miss Sally might even have his formula beat."

Dillie laughs at that. "I won't. Are your dad's meals as delicious as the ones he makes for Wednesday night dinner?"

"Yup." I nod. "Especially the lasagna."

"Mmm. You have access to the best food. Clearly, I love to eat." She laughs as she blows a little on a curly fry, then chews it while she gets to work mixing her ketchup, mayo, and mustard together. "It's so funny that we have the same exact order, though. Even down to the ketchup mix."

"Told you," I say, mixing my own condiments. "When I saw your LiveClip, I knew you had to come here, especially after realizing we order the same thing. That's—that's why I wanted to order for you. As a matter of fact, I was sitting right here when I was watching it."

"Really?" Her eyes grow wide again. "Were you here by yourself?"

"No. It was me, Justin, and his cousin."

"Y'all were all just eating and watching my live?" Her grin slowly creeps across her face. Dangerous territory.

"We were just trying to see—"

I watch every live, listen to every podcast . . .

"—if you'd found out who the mystery singer was."

Why would I say that? If I was in dangerous territory before, I'd just taken another step closer.

Dillie takes a big bite of her burger, and another, before she stands up and claps, playfully.

Sally looks over and smiles.

"You like it, huh?" I ask.

"This is the best burger I've ever had! Like ever. It's better than the ones my daddy makes right off the grill." She whips her head toward me. "Don't worry, I'll keep your secret."

I nod. "Deal."

Miss Sally beams, her round eyes crinkle. "I'm glad you like it, Dillie. Now, finish up so I can send y'all on your way with some ice cream."

Dillie sits back down and finishes her burger, and for a few minutes, we just eat in silence. That's why Sally's is always so quiet. You want to spend all your time savoring your food.

After we both finish our burgers and Dillie is still working on her fries, Sally brings over two vanilla ice cream cones. I'm almost too full to eat mine but I can't resist. Dillie takes one of her curly fries and dips it into her ice cream.

"I still don't know who the mystery singer is, if you were still wondering," Dillie says as she chews. "I mean, some of my friends think it's Miles, especially because of that amazing performance he had last night at the Fall Choral Concert."

I feel a twinge of something again . . . jealousy? Or maybe regret, or wistfulness, wishing I was singing my own solo with my own arrangements.

"It . . . could be him" is all I say. I take a bite of my ice cream. "I guess you'll find out when he wins, right?" I can't help but pry.

My heart thumps. Dillie takes three fries and dips them into her ice cream again, chews, and swallows. Then she shrugs. "Yeah, I guess so."

I furrow my brow. "Is something wrong?"

"Can I tell you something else? I can trust you, right?"

I nod so fast my head begins to hurt. "Of course."

She leans in closer, the smell of the ice cream mixing in with her vanilla perfume.

"I know the song is popular and everything . . . but I actually don't like it."

15: B-Side

She doesn't like it?

Delia doesn't like my song?

The song where I poured out my feelings to her?

This must be how Jerrod feels. Suddenly, I have sympathy for him. As terrible of a rapper he is, he still loves it and it must've hurt to hear Destiny say that he can't stay on beat.

I picture me and Delia together, me in the studio singing loudly, giving it all my might.

I take off my headphones. The engineer stands up and claps. "Bravo, Darren. You really knocked it out of the park."

I look at Delia, anxiously. "So? What do you think?"

She smiles at me sadly, and shakes her head. "I'm sorry, Darren. I just don't like it."

"What didn't you like about it?" I ask her. "Tell me. Was it my voice? The lyrics?"

"Everything," she says. "You just aren't the singer you thought you were."

"Darren?" Dillie says. "Are you okay?"

I blink and realize where I am—Sally's. Dillie's beside me, still eating her ice cream cone. I can't believe I just had another Delia Daydream while real-life Delia is right beside me.

I can't believe that she doesn't like my song.

I think about the Clip comments, the song blaring out of the car speakers I hear every day. How silly I was to think that it would actually win the contest.

Because none of this matters if the person I wrote it for doesn't even like it.

"I'm sorry, I was just . . . thinking," I tell her. "What don't you like about the mystery singer's song?" A part of me wants to retreat back into my head forever. But it's different with music, especially when it's *my* music. If I don't know the answer for sure, I will make up a million reasons why she didn't. I have to know.

"It's just . . ." She sighs a little bit and bites her lip. "The song is supposed to be about me, right? And at first, I was flattered, like who wouldn't be? But then I thought to myself . . . this guy might not even know me. He might not feel that way if he *did* know me. I mean, I leave hair in the drain on wash day and share clothes with my little sister."

Hair in the drain? I shudder a little bit. Instantly, I'm taken back to the countless arguments Zoe and I had about her hair everywhere when we shared a bathroom.

"He said he was mesmerized by my hips and thighs, but would he be if he knew I had stretch marks or a huge scar from when I fell off my bike in middle school?"

"Stretch marks aren't a big deal," I say, at least feeling confident about that. "And who doesn't have a huge scar from middle school?"

"But I've been self-conscious about mine since I got them," she admits, "and who's to say the mystery singer doesn't feel the same way?" She sighs again. "It makes me feel like a fraud when I listen to the song."

I stare at Dillie, really seeing her. I can't believe she has things she is insecure about, as beautiful as she is. She catches me staring and looks away.

"I'm oversharing again," she says, kind of to me but mostly to herself.

I'm taken back to what her sister said at the Rockin' Lock-In: *That's easy for you to say. You can just edit out the parts when you mess up on your show.*

I wonder how many thoughts she edits out of her podcast?

"No it's—it's fine. You're not oversharing. You're just . . . sharing." I kind of admire it, the openness with which she shares her flaws—or what she sees as flaws.

"Well, it's not just that." Dillie keeps going. "The song, on a technical level, is really good. Even if it wasn't about me, you know? But . . . I'm not sure that it fits my podcast. It's a little too slow to be the theme song, I think."

"Really?" I frown, and it sends a small pang to the pit of my stomach. Or maybe that's the heavy burger I just ate. So Justin and Jerrod were right after all.

"Yeah. I was reading some Clip Messages last night and some people agree. I mean, most people like it, but the people who don't say it's too slow, kind of boring . . ."

Each critique feels like a punch in the stomach. These were my real feelings that people were calling slow and boring. I put it all out there.

"And even though the lyrics are pretty, and that guy can sing, he's not even coming forward about it. I don't want to pronounce him the winner if I don't even know whether it's real. It's weird. I love the idea of the song and those lyrics are super sweet and thoughtful but . . . don't you think he'd come forward by now to claim them? Like, how long does he think I'm going to wait?"

Somewhere in the back of my mind, phantom Justin is telling me, "I told you so."

"Yeah, I get that" is all I say.

I glance at my phone. It's almost time for the first bell to ring. I don't even know what to think.

Maybe we should've gone with the fast version of the song after all. But . . . I didn't like it. Was it worth it to have a song that I didn't like, that Dillie and her listeners liked?

And then she said the mystery singer doesn't know her. When I'm right here, right now, trying to get to know her.

What if she knew it was me? Would that change her mind? Should I tell her now?

No. Not if she already admitted to me she doesn't like it. I can't say anything yet.

"We should head back," I say. "Mrs. Jones has no mercy when it comes to tardies."

"Tell me about it. I have her first thing in the morning." Dillie rolls her eyes at the thought. "She doesn't even have mercy when you're late because of *traffic*. Anyway." She smiles again. "Thanks for the burger, Darren. Miss Sally can consider me a new paying customer."

"You'll never look at another burger again," I say, putting Miss Sally's tip on the table and waving to her as she helps another customer.

I'm still working on my ice cream and trying to carry both Dillie's drink and mine in my hand when we walk to the front. I shift everything to one hand to open the door for her, but she runs in front of me and pulls it.

"Do you think you're an octopus?" She laughs as the door swings open and grabs her drink, the one with red lipstick around the rim of the straw.

On the way back, the Louis Dot song plays on the radio *again*, and Dillie sings along, while I replay the lunch in my head.

I poured out my heart to Dillie and she didn't even like it.

This is what I get for being vulnerable.

Things were much safer in my head.

16: Queen Charming

"This week has been a whirlwind. I've gotten so many fake submissions claiming to be the mystery singer. Is this how Prince Charming felt when trying to find the *real* owner of the glass slipper? Just call me Princess Charming. Or Queen Charming? I like the sound of that."

It's Sunday, and I'm lying in bed, prepped for my Sunday nap, listening to Dillie's show to hear the winner of the contest. Since Dillie hates the song, I'm sure it won't be me, but I at least want to hear if the person who did win was any good.

It wasn't a big deal anyway. Just a song I wrote on a whim that was sent in by Jerrod. Now I don't have to tell her it was me at all. The song and its popularity will eventually fade away.

There is something sad about this. Finally, I was able to sing without the unwanted critique and potential embarrassment from others. And now that's gone.

My song still had critiques, even though it was pretty popular. I guess even if you're anonymous, there's no way around it. And she didn't like it, so what was the point? I guess it's for the best, then, if the song fades into obscurity.

I know that Justin will remind me that I still haven't asked Dillie out now that I don't have the mystery singer thing to hide behind. But still . . .

We'll cross that bridge when we get to it.

"I guess it's time for Queen Charming to unveil the Cinderfella who won the contest. Wow, that was corny. Let's get to the winner for the contest before I lose any subscribers over it. Okay, drumroll please."

A soundbite of a drumroll fills the speakers.

"And the winner of the *Dillie D in the Place to Be* Mystery Song Contest is . . ."

I glance over at the Bluetooth speaker.

She laughs, a cross between a yell and a scoff. "It's everyone's favorite anonymous song!"

I sit up in bed and look at my speaker. What?

An applause track plays, followed by the beginning of my song. *"Stop whatever you're doing . . ."*

"Y'all really love this one! Anyway, the prize is for him to come on the show and be interviewed. And I don't even know who he is. So, mystery singer, come forward! I've emailed him back, so only time will tell. I must admit, I'm a little intrigued. I hope he's cute."

I stare at my speaker in disbelief. Why did my song win when Dillie told me she couldn't stand it?

"If you don't tell her it's you at this point, you are ridiculous. It's that simple."

This is how Justin greets me when I open the door later this evening. He usually eats Sunday dinner at his house, but his parents are on a cruise celebrating their twenty-fifth wedding anniversary, so I invited him over earlier this week.

Clearly, that was a mistake.

"My Sunday is going great, how's yours?" I ask as we walk to the dining room.

"I'm serious."

I'm just confused. Dillie opened up and told me why she didn't like the song. So, why did it win? I make (another) mistake by asking Justin this.

"You gotta give the people what they want," he says. "Her Clip followers are probably mostly listeners of her show, or potential listeners. If it wins, they'll be more likely to tune in. End of story. Now you gotta tell her you're the mystery singer and ask her out."

"But she didn't even like the song," I tell him.

"So?" He shrugs. "Tiffany doesn't like my new haircut. What does that have to do with anything?"

I eye Justin's haircut. I personally wouldn't have picked it for his head shape, but it's no skin off my bones.

"You can't compare a haircut to me literally putting out there how I feel about her," I argue.

"Why can't I? Tiffany saw me and immediately told me she hated my haircut. I *know* it's fly so I don't care. Dillie doesn't even know that you wrote the song. So what does any of this have to do with you asking her out?"

Because music is how I express myself. And if she doesn't like my music, how can she like me? I ask myself as I stare at Justin's lopsided cut. Music speaks when I can't. And what that song said, Dillie didn't even like.

I did enjoy that studio session, but I don't know if that, or potentially getting rejected by Dillie, was worth the heartbreak.

"Hey, honey!" My mom greets Justin, oven mitts on her hands. Since Dad is a chef, he usually does the cooking, but every so often my mom will get in there and do her thang. Her soul food thang, to be exact. "The food is almost ready, boys."

My stomach growls as we follow her into the dining room.

We say grace around the table and it's silent as we eat the meal of chicken, macaroni and cheese, corn bread, string beans, collard greens, yams, and rice and gravy.

"So, what are you up to, Justin?" my mom asks. "Did you and Darren finish your project?"

"Project?" Justin's brow furrows.

"The studio," I mutter.

"Oh, yes we did."

She looks from Justin to me. "Was it not a project?"

"It was something like that," I say as Justin opens his mouth. "It just . . . wasn't for school."

"Well, what was it for?" She eyes us both with her big brown eyes.

Oh, no.

"It—I was recording a song. For a contest." I say this as fast as I can, but Mom catches the word *song*, anyway.

"Oh. You were *singing*?"

"What was the contest for, son?" Dad asks, coming up for air after finishing the last bite on his plate and reaching for another piece of corn bread.

I can feel Justin getting ready to share everything with my dad. At least if I do it on my own, I can tell the truth and get ahead of my own story.

"It was for Dillie's podcast. She picks a winner and will use that song as her theme song and interview the artist on her show."

My parents look at each other in poorly concealed excitement, raising their eyebrows and smirking at each other, then trying to fix their faces back into neutral territory. This makes me think they have been talking about wanting me to sing again and didn't want to get their hopes up or let on that they've been discussing me.

Dad clears his throat. "Well, that's . . . great. I'm glad you're using your gift again." He hesitates, chooses his next words carefully. "What made you decide to enter?"

"Love will make you leap," my mom says, smiling to herself, cutting into her piece of chicken. She looks up and realizes that we are staring at her.

"I mean . . . I was talking about your love for singing, not Delia." She smirks. "But like will make you leap, too."

"Hey, son." Dad looks at me like a light bulb just went off over his head. "If you win the contest, that's a perfect way to talk to Delia and tell her how you feel."

My eyes widen in mock surprise as if I hadn't heard or thought of this at all before, and kick Justin under the table to let him know not to tell my parents I won. The prospect of me entering *and* winning a singing contest would be enough for my parents to pack their bags and hand deliver me to every Broadway audition they can find.

Mom nods enthusiastically.

"Yeah!" Dad continues. "Sing your feelings. That's what's wrong with today's R&B—these cats don't know how to sing their *feelings*. They don't know how to put their feelings on the *line*." He hits the table for emphasis. "Too afraid of getting rejected and not looking cool, when some of the coolest have put their feelings out there. Look at Usher, Dru Hill, Shai . . ."

Dad's looking straight at me, and I'm fighting the urge to roll my eyes. *Everything* must always go back to nineties R&B to him. Let him tell it (and trust me, he will), nineties R&B played a huge part in the early days of him dating my mom.

"Well, I wouldn't say all of that," Justin says. "I feel like some artists of our generation know how to sing about love. Look at Louis Dot Williams for example."

I make a face while Dad rubs his chin. "Okay, I'll give that young man props. His lyrics are nice but . . ."

"He can't sing all that well, in my opinion." I take a sip of sweet tea. I think about what Dillie said, that she could feel the emotion in his song. "Even if he, uh, is relatable to a lot of people."

"Exactly," Dad says.

"Kevin Crooner?" Justin presses.

Dad scrunches up his nose. "To me, it seems like he talks about how many women he can two-time than real romance."

Justin looks at me with a confused expression. "Two-time?"

"It means to cheat or to be unfaithful, but in parent language," I explain.

The conversation goes on for a bit, and it makes me realize that Dad and I have the same idea of what constitutes a good R&B song: great lyrics, even better singing, abstract harmonies, a strong bridge. No one can resist a good nineties R&B song. I feel like I hit all the points with my own song, which is probably why I like it.

I realize that Dillie and some other people may not like my song, but I still like it. Even if it is boring, or too slow to be the theme song for her show. Something about that thought lifts an invisible weight off my shoulders.

Soon, dinner is over and Justin and I help my parents clean off the table and pack up leftovers.

"Remember. If you don't tell Dillie you won, you are ridiculous," Justin repeats again on his way out. "You can't make any more excuses this time." His phone buzzes, and a picture of Justin and Tiffany pops up. He grins.

"I'm outta here."

"Don't get caught. Again," I say, raising my eyebrow. The last time Justin snuck Tiffany into his house, he got caught and got in trouble, which means *I* got caught and got in trouble, because I covered for him.

"I won't. Well, I'll try not to. What are you about to do?"

"Just chill."

Justin shakes his head. "You could be doing what I'm about to do right now, but with Dillie."

"You mean face a guaranteed grounding once you inevitably get caught?"

Justin shrugs. "It's worth it. Plus, I won't get caught this time. My parents are probably sipping daiquiris on an island right now."

I glance at my parents' bedroom, the downstairs primary, right beside the stairs. Not a chance. "I don't even know if she'd be up for that." For any of this, really.

"You won't know until you ask, will you? She's not going to come meet you in your head."

I say nothing. Justin answers the phone to speak to Tiffany and waves distractedly as he leaves the house. I hear my parents laughing at something in their room and walk upstairs.

I scroll on my phone for a second, then replay a little of Dillie's newest podcast episode.

The fact is this: even though she didn't like the song, it still won the contest. I told Justin and Jerrod I'd cross this bridge when I came to it.

I'm here, and don't know which way to go.

17: Ghostwriter

"There she is, dawg," Justin says.

We're headed down the hallway, and Dillie is about to walk past my locker. Tiffany appears and she and Justin walk away together.

I'm vaguely wondering if Dillie thinks I'm attractive. I think I am, and I've heard from Zoe's friends and my Clip Messages that other girls think that, too. But what about *her*?

She gives me an amused look, one that seems so intense I start to wonder if I'm doing something funny.

We meet, my locker in between us.

"What's up, Dillie?" I say, quickly doing my combination and hoping it's not one of the rare times it gets jammed on the first try.

"Hey! So, I announced a winner last night," she says, with a playful eye roll.

"I—heard." I trip over my words after realizing that she doesn't know it's me.

Duh, Darren. How would she know?

I should say something else, so she *really* doesn't know it's me.

"Did he reveal himself?"

She shakes her head.

"How are you going to interview him?"

She sighs, puts her back against the locker beside me. "I'm going to wait to see if he comes forward first. If not, I'm thinking of just sending an email to the address, with a date, time, and no excuses."

Date, time, and no excuse. I try to picture me showing up for the interview, and what her initial reaction might be. Shock? Anger? Was Justin right, and I'm dragging this out too long? Maybe it's too late to say anything. Or maybe this deadline is just the push I need.

"That sounds like a plan."

"Yeah. That's if I don't get tired of this first. I gotta admit, it's kind of fun. But I could see myself getting annoyed by this after a while. Is it a gimmick to create buzz around his name? Or is he just that shy? Or what if it's all a joke? I don't want to waste my time."

My stomach gives a jolt. "I feel that, though. Um . . ." I lower my voice. "How did the song win, if you said you didn't like it?"

Dillie's smile falters a bit, not meeting her eyes as much as it did a few seconds before.

She shrugs. "You gotta give the people what they want, right?"

I glance backward to make sure that Justin didn't walk by, or I'd never hear the end of it.

"I guess," I say, then shake my head. "But you didn't like it at all. Can you overrule it somehow? I mean, it *is* your show."

"Of course it's my show," Dillie snaps, and I instantly get the feeling that I struck a nerve. "But that's exactly it. If most of my listeners like that song, it *has* to win. I get messages every day about it, people hoping it's the one I chose. It's what they will hear every time they stream my podcast. I need them to at least like the theme song, so when I start introducing my mentorship content, they—they can at least like *something*."

She looks away again, but I can see on her face the same expression she had when she talked about her podcast at the Rockin' Lock-In.

I choose my words wisely. Dillie is so open, maybe she won't mind if I say this. "You said you wanted to be a role model, right? Well . . . what message does that send if you're going along with something you don't even like, just so you can have more listeners? Like, isn't that the one thing we all struggle with in high school? Doing things we don't like, just to be liked?"

I can't believe I'm saying this about my *own* song.

I can't believe I'm saying any of this. But I'm realizing with every opinion I say, I'm getting to know Dillie. Her insecurities, what makes her laugh, what makes her annoyed. It's enough to fuel my Delia Daydreams, but it's also enough to make me stay with her in the present.

She looks at me for a second, her eyes flickering up and down across my face.

"You don't get it." She hikes her book bag up on her back. "I know that you're going through something with your passion, whatever it is, but I don't want to go through that with mine. My podcast is on the up and up, and I want to keep it that way."

"It's not bad to go through something with your passion," I say, surprising myself. This is the first time I've voiced this out loud. "Sometimes it helps to take a step back to see what really matters."

"Well, I don't want to take a step back," she says, and then, ironically, takes a step back. We both look down at her feet, and I laugh, a nervous one.

"Are you sure about that?" I try to dissolve the tension.

The bell rings.

She only smiles a little bit, then shakes her head. "You're funny, Darren. I'll see you later." None of these conversations ever go the way they do in my Delia Daydreams. But I still don't want them to end.

"I'm sure you'll find out soon enough," I call out as she walks away, not even trusting my own words.

She looks back. "Yeah. The truth always comes to light. One way or another."

"What do you mean you're not going to tell her?"

It's Saturday night, and Justin is spending the night at my house. He went to a party with Tiffany and after too many times breaking it, his curfew is way earlier than mine. He asked his mom if he could spend the night here, so after leaving the party (late) with Tiffany, he made his way up to my room, disrupting my night with yet another question.

I just shrug. What's the point? I still like my song, but it would be weird to say something to her now, as much as we've talked about who the mystery singer could be. Especially since she's not a fan.

And although I'm not entirely sure, I think we're starting to make a connection. Now, I don't even need the song. Right?

I tell Justin this, and he shakes his head.

"It's not just about Dillie, though. You're going to let the song fade away without any credit?"

"Why not?" I ask. "It was something we put together in the studio for that contest. No big deal. The song will be played out in a week or so."

Even as I say the words, something about them doesn't feel natural. What's coming out of my mouth and what's in my heart aren't connecting.

"Look, Darren. I know the song was sleepy and a little boring"—I grimace at that—"but everyone was saying you sounded good. You could do *something* with it. Matter of fact, this could be your new thing. Singing. Well, your old thing, since you've *been* singing."

Justin has this incredulous look on his face, and a small part of me gets it. I *do* like to sing. I love to sing. This would be the perfect way to slide back into that groove. I picture myself in the studio again, doing something more than a jingle. I could stop critiquing the music that's on the radio and apply my notes to my own music.

But it wouldn't be just that. It'd be people critiquing my voice, asking me to sing everywhere, giving unsolicited opinions on what I should do next or how I sound. I could get booed again. In my head, in my car, in the shower, in my room, I could sing without all that. Once I started singing publicly, the magic would be tainted again.

"Anyway, something happened with Tiffany and I want your advice." Justin changes the subject. "She's trippin'. Was I wrong for . . ."

I try to listen, but I keep thinking about what Justin said. I know how well I can sing, and sometimes it feels strange to even *say that*.

What if I get a record deal immediately and am thrust into a world of isolated fame?

Or what if this is a stepping-stone to making music at my own pace?

What if people continue to criticize my voice or misunderstand when I have a cold and I'm not actually losing my voice?

Or what if I inspire someone else, like Tara?

All I know is "Dillie's Song" will die down, people will forget about it, and I can be back in my head, safe and sound.

Though, is there a possibility that I should just . . . let it out and see what happens?

"Darren? Was I wrong?" he asks.

I was so lost in thought, I didn't hear a single thing he said.

"I don't know" is all I say, the most truthful answer I can give.

18: Deep Cut

My mama has a hard rule that if you spend the night on Saturday, you have to come with us to church on Sunday, so Justin and I take my car to church in the morning. I have welcome committee this morning, so Justin hangs around the front door with me while I pass out coffee and doughnuts to everyone, and mini-Bibles and car decals that say GOD LOVES YOU. YES, *YOU*! to new visitors. It's the early service, so I take a little coffee for myself, even though it's bitter for my taste. I prefer sweet tea.

"Hi, Darren." I hear a familiar voice behind me. I turn around to see Dillie holding a cup of coffee from a local café. Her hair is up in a bun, with tiny curls falling down in the back, and she's wearing glasses. I don't think I've ever seen her in glasses before.

"Dillie," I say, after I hand a new visiting couple in front of me two Bibles and two decals. "You're here early. Nice glasses."

She touches them absentmindedly. "Thanks. I kind of hate them, but I broke my favorite pair last week and my eyes are too dry for contacts. I'm tired this morning." She registers Justin sitting down beside the welcome table and gives him a wave. I can't tell what he does, because my back is to him and I don't want to see him shooting me any type of looks, trying to coach me on what to do or say.

"Tell me about it," I say, pausing to greet two men with blue hair and approximately one million facial piercings between them. "This is the one time I actually considered drinking coffee."

"Wait." She holds up her empty hand. "Hold up. You don't drink coffee?"

I give a few kids the children's church program and a small box of crayons. "Nope. I just tried this one and—"

"Oh, well you can't judge *this* coffee," she says, after she looks around and makes sure no one is listening. "No offense, but it's not that good. It's just something for the people who forgot to pick up coffee on the way here, I think. You need to try Nonna's down the street."

"Is that where you went?" I ask. Service will be starting soon, so fewer and fewer people are coming to the welcome table.

She nods excitedly. "Are you busy after church? I was going to stop by again afterward to pick up a croissant. You can come with me."

"I'm not busy," I say quickly, surprising myself. I've been finding myself barely holding my thoughts back about music, but now I'm noticing when it comes to Dillie, I'm speaking more and more without overthinking, too. Truthfully, Justin and I were going to meet Jerrod to play basketball later, but they've both canceled plans with me for their girlfriends a bunch of times, so I figure they owe me one, anyway.

Not that Dillie is my girlfriend, of course.

"Cool. I'll text you after service is over." She takes a sip and flounces away to the doors that lead to the chapel.

I look over at Justin, to see if he has his usual notes on how I should've handled the situation, but instead, he looks oddly impressed.

"It's happening for you, man," he says. "Don't mess it up."

Riding in the passenger seat of Dillie's car is an experience. The inside smells like strawberries, and her back seat is cluttered with different pairs of shoes, books, and various other items. When she unlocks the car door, a wave of heat comes out. The steering wheel has a cheetah print covering over it. When she cranks up the car, a Beyoncé song picks up where it left off.

"Nonna's is so good," Dillie says as she pulls onto the street.

I told my parents I'll meet them at home, and my mom shot me a knowing look, because moms just *know*. I also gave Justin the keys to drive my car home and pick up his own. I am not sure my mom knows this, though, because she probably wouldn't have allowed it.

"Don't be offended if I don't like it," I say. "I'm not a coffee drinker." My sister frequents one of the chains around here. She forced me to try hers one time and then got mad and told me I wasted her precious coffee when I spit it out.

Dillie glances over at me and says nothing; she just smiles to herself.

"Did you enjoy the service this morning?" she asks.

I nod. Ironically, the sermon was about identifying and using your spiritual gifts.

"What do you think your spiritual gift is? I think mine would be talking to people. I know it sounds silly but you know your theory about listening? I feel like sometimes when you talk to people and make them feel super comfortable, they'll share something vulnerable and you can help them through it, you know? That's why I want to start having people on my podcast."

I nod again. "That's good logic. I guess the main thing is making the other person comfortable enough to have the floor. You're good at that," I muse, after thinking about the awkward but interesting conversations we've been having.

"Right," she says quietly. "What's your spiritual gift?" she asks again.

The word *S I N G I N G* instinctively pops into my head. I think about when I used to sing in church, how the old ladies would be so proud of me. How my mom would cry tears of joy, every single time. It made people happy. It helped me say exactly what I wanted to say, without overthinking anything.

Regardless of people's opinions, whether or not I was using too much vibrato or too many runs, whether I was singing too loudly or too softly, whenever I sang, I felt connected, like I was doing what I was supposed to do.

"My spiritual gift . . ." I start to say, then decide to change the subject when a question pops into my head. Maybe one Dillie can help me with. "Can I ask you a question?"

"Sure."

"You love *Dillie D in the Place to Be*, right?"

"It's my favorite thing in the world to do right now."

"How do you . . . handle the criticism you get about the show? Like the sweet tea, and . . . stuff."

She thinks about this for a second, as she turns onto the street with the tall sign that says "Nonna's" at the end of it.

"Can I tell you a secret?" she asks.

"Sure." *Dillie trusts me to keep a secret*, I think. I can't help but beam at this realization.

"When I first started *Dillie D*, I almost quit after the first episode."

"Why?" I ask. I'm shocked. I had no idea.

"Well . . . okay, so I made my first episode as a release from a bad breakup. I wasn't talking about the breakup specifically, but the topic was relationships. My ex-boyfriend is popular, so of course, I saw a bunch of Clip comments saying I was trying to get attention, that I was doing this to get him back—which is ridiculous because I'd *never* want him back—that nobody wants to hear this show, blah blah blah . . . Something that was supposed to be an outlet got into the hands of a bunch of people who didn't care about what I wanted to do. It wasn't for them, and they didn't understand it, but I felt like my little show was . . ."

"Tainted?" I offer. I feel angry for her—at this ex-boyfriend who broke her heart, at these people making opinions when they don't know the entire story. It would be enough to make anyone want to quit.

"Yeah." She glances over at me before she parks the car. "Exactly. So . . . I almost stopped. But then I thought, you know what? People are going to say what they want to say about me anyway. The people who are supposed to get it, get it. I do exactly what I want to do on that show, but when it goes live . . . that's it. It's out of my hands. It's mine, but I can't control what people think, and art is meant to be shared, you know?"

She parks the car, turns it off, and looks me in the eyes.

"Yeah. That makes a lot of sense."

This makes me think about my sister, Zoe. Even when she was little, she was good at virtually everything she set out to do—she won so many awards, contests, pageants. She was liked by so many, but I remember the early days, when she'd come home from school crying that someone bullied her because of it. I felt like maybe they were just a little jealous, wanted a piece of her spotlight. Maybe the same thing happened to Dillie.

"You say he—your ex—is popular, but you're popular, too," I point out. "Maybe he was the one who was trying to get popular off of your show." I picture it, some guy bragging that he broke up with The Delia Dawson. The thought makes my stomach drop in disgust.

She scoffs, and I wonder if I've said the wrong thing. "I'm not—I wasn't really popular at my old school," she says, and shrugs.

I cock my head to one side. I can't imagine a school—or even a world—where Dillie's presence doesn't command the attention of everyone around her.

"I just find that hard to believe." I smile a little, but then look away before she thinks I'm weird for staring.

"I'm serious!" She giggles a little. "People always said I was annoying or extra. I don't know if you've picked up on this, Darren, but I talk a lot. I guess some people call it word vomit? Why do you think I started a podcast talking to myself? Sometimes I get really excited and meet new friends and open up to them and then . . ." She shakes her head, like she just came out of a daydream. It's funny—while I think through my daydreams, she seems to talk through them. "You'd think I'd learn by now." She laughs again, but this time it has an air of sadness to it. "Delia Dawson isn't the popular one. Dillie D is."

She glances at me, a beat longer than I thought she would. I try to pull my car door open, but it's locked.

She sighs. "Speaking of popular . . . It's just hard now because . . . when I first started, people already had it out for me, so I felt less pressure to do what they wanted. But now that the show is getting popular . . . I feel like I have an obligation to give them what they ask for at least *some* of the time. I don't know. I keep going back and forth." She gets that look again, the same one she gets every time she talks about what to do about her potential podcast changes.

"Patricia doesn't open from the inside on the passenger side. The lock gets jammed," she says, referring to her car, her face tinting pink. She adjusts her glasses quickly as she turns to open her own door.

She looks back, winks, and says, "I guess I can return the favor from Sally's."

She walks over and opens my door, and together we walk into Nonna's. Everything—the furniture, the floors—is made of some type of dark wood, and there are big plants everywhere. I hear a saxophone blowing softly from somewhere farther inside.

There's no line, and the people inside are already seated and reading, talking across a table to someone, or typing on their computers, each with a mug of coffee. I didn't even know coffee shops *had* real dishes.

We walk up to the counter, where a woman with black fluffy hair is standing.

"Back again?" she says, and although she's smirking, I can instantly tell she's not someone to play with.

Dillie nods, then grabs my arm and squeezes it. My stomach flips at the touch.

"Not for me," Dillie says. "This is Darren. He doesn't like coffee. Or so he says."

Dillie and Nonna say, "Or so he says" at the same time. I look around, wondering if that's the slogan of this place.

"I'll make you a small cup." Nonna turns around, grabbing cups and scooping coffee beans.

"Let's sit." Dillie points to the small table with two chairs across from each other.

"It smells good in here," I say. I'm usually indifferent to the smell of coffee, but combined with the smell of buttery croissants, it actually smells nice.

"Just wait until you taste it. It'll be ten times better than what you think."

In a few minutes, Nonna comes to our table with a small mug of coffee, two glasses of water, and a huge chocolate croissant.

"To share." She half smirks again, then goes back behind the counter.

"Go ahead," Dillie says. Her eyes are dancing, bright—like she's ready to say, "I told you so."

I taste the coffee and a pleasant sensation goes through my body. It's sweet and warm. I take a few more sips and I'm instantly a little more alert, but not jittery like I was with my sister's coffee.

"Good, right?" she says. She's studying me and the cup, taking me in. I know the look—it's the same one I get when I'm trying to remember every single detail in a moment to take home and roll around in my head at night. The only difference is, Dillie's thoughts are itching to get out. To be talked about.

I nod. "Yeah. Now I feel like every other sip of coffee I had before was fake coffee."

"*Exactly!* Nonna is so intentional with every cup she makes. Nothing is ever thrown together. This isn't the place you come when you're in a rush."

I take another sip and nod, licking the foam from my lips. The movement catches her eye, but only for a second.

"That's my spiritual gift, I think."

"What? Deciphering good coffee from bad coffee?" She snickers. "Don't get ahead of yourself."

"Nah," I say, taking another sip. The cup was so small, it's almost gone. "Being intentional. Deliberate. Rational. I don't do a lot of things without thinking about them first. My mama said it made me the most patient baby." I chuckle. "But it does have its downside because I don't have a lot of practice in making split-second decisions."

I can't believe I'm saying these things to Dillie, while draining a cup of coffee, no less. But voicing out loud the thoughts that have been piling up feels like a release. I can see if I'm alone in thinking them, or not. It frees up some space for the big thoughts, like a decluttering of the room in my mind.

"But what about when you have to make one?" Dillie asks. She balls up her fists and sets her chin in the palms of her hands. "A split-second decision. What do you do?"

"I pretty much try to avoid them at all costs. I know, it's bad," I add when she raises an eyebrow at me. I think back to missing the karaoke session at the lock-in, all the times I thought "What if" instead of "What I could've done better." "If something doesn't feel right, I won't do it until it does."

"But how do you know if something feels wrong, or if you're just trying to talk yourself out of something that feels right?"

"I—don't," I say. Wow. "I guess the only way to know is to at least try."

Dillie gives me the satisfied look of someone who just helped you realize something about yourself. "Exactly," she says. "You were all 'take a step back' when really, *you* need to 'take a step *forward*'!" She laughs.

"Take a step forward about what?" I ask. My heart beats fast. She couldn't be . . . talking about . . . us, as a couple . . . could she?

"You know . . . that passion that you're taking a break from. What is it anyway? Running track or something?"

I am just about to tell her it's singing when I realize—if she knows that I am rediscovering how I feel about singing, will she put together that I am the mystery singer?

Maybe this is the time to tell the truth. We have been sitting here, drinking coffee, sharing secrets. It feels right . . . almost. But everything is going so well in this moment . . . revealing the truth would change everything. What should I do? There is no one to ask, but me. Not Justin, not Jerrod, not my mom.

She just said take a step forward. I realize there's no way to know if something's right without trying. Maybe this is the first step in the right direction—

"Hello! Earth to Darren!" Dillie waves a hand in front of my face. She laughs when my eyes focus on her. "What is that passion of yours? I'm not letting you get out of telling me that easily."

"Oh um . . . art." When I say it, I don't feel the sense of relief that I usually do when I keep something in my head. Instantly, I know I made the wrong choice.

"Oh! Like sculpting? Yeah, I guess I could see how sculpting could be hard if you don't have inspiration."

"No . . . more like . . . painting. Painting . . . pictures." I keep going deeper and deeper into this non-truth, without knowing why, really. I guess I'm doing what I've always done—keeping my thoughts to myself—but for some reason, in this moment, it feels foreign to me.

"Ooh." She takes a sip of her coffee and she starts talking as soon as she swallows it. "Maybe you need a muse."

"A muse?" I say. The word sparks an unexplainable light in my brain, an idea that I tuck away for later.

"Yeah, you know. Someone to inspire you to paint again."

I already have one, I think, looking at the beautiful curly-haired girl in front of me.

The silence draws on for a second and I drain the rest of my coffee. "That was really good. I might even skip my Sunday nap."

"No amount of coffee will make me skip my Sunday nap." She pulls the croissant a little closer to her. "May I? She said we could share it."

"Go ahead," I say, then grab the other side of it. We each pull until it comes apart, some of the chocolate falling on the round dish.

I take a bite at the same time Dillie does. Buttery, flaky, chocolaty, soft. The best croissant I've had in a long time.

Only . . . I know that I have some in my teeth.

"Do I have chocolate on my nose?" Dillie asks, wiggling her nose around, squinching and un-squinching it. "I can feel it."

"Yeah," I say, trying to hide the chocolate that's definitely on my teeth. She wipes her nose, but the swipe makes the chocolate spot bigger.

"Here." I grab a napkin and give it to her.

"Can you get it?" She giggles, but her eyes flicker everywhere around her. I can't tell if she's embarrassed or something else I can't read.

"Sure." The chocolate is kind of drying on her nose, so I dab a little water on it from the water glass on the table, just enough to dampen it, and wipe it off. I work carefully, taking in the moment.

It's an awkward motion and the woman at the counter eyes us quizzically. Dillie is still squinching her nose, blinking faster the closer my hands get to her face. She laughs, but it fades away as I gently brush the napkin across her nose. I realize I'm holding her chin. That we're close enough to kiss.

She must realize this at the same time because her eyes open and we just stare at each other. And we move closer and closer to each other.

The clanking of a nearby dish snaps me out of it.

"Um, the chocolate is gone," I confirm, leaning back into my seat.

"Thanks," she replies, quietly. She looks down and up at me again.

At that moment, I realize something is different.

We're in Dillie's car, in my neighborhood, about to turn onto the street where my house is. There's a new energy in the air I can't put my finger on. Most of the car ride is quiet, besides occasional comments about the songs that come on the radio.

She approaches my house and I groan as I see my mom outside, watering the flowers on our front porch. My mom is nosy and there is a one hundred percent chance that she'll walk up to the car.

As Dillie turns into the driveway, my mom watches us. We make eye contact, but I can tell she's unsure who's driving. She walks straight to me. I roll the window down.

"Darren, why did you have Justin drive your car home? He is not on our insurance—" She stops her lecture as she sees exactly who's driving.

"Hi, Mrs. Armstrong," Dillie says. "I was just dropping Darren off. I wanted him to try this coffee place that I love."

"Coffee?" Mama eyes me curiously. "And you liked it?"

"It was pretty good." I nod. Mama looks at me, then Dillie, then me again.

"Sorry for letting Justin drive the car, Mama," I say.

"It's okay," my mama says, an air in her voice that lets me know she has more questions when we get in the house. "He's still here; I told him he could stay for dinner. Your father is trying a new recipe tonight."

"I heard Mr. Armstrong makes a mean lasagna," Dillie says. "That's one of my favorite foods."

"Oh, yes, he does." Mama smiles. "Maybe you can come over next time he makes it."

Did my mama just invite Dillie over for dinner?

She winks at Dillie.

What is going on?

"Oh, I'll have to make sure Darren tells me ahead of time," Dillie says.

"You can stay tonight if you'd like. It's a casserole, so there will be more than enough to go around."

Mama is always inviting people over for dinner but this is . . . different.

Dillie just sighs. "I wish I could, but I have to go home and do some last-minute work on my podcast before it goes live. Darren, let me know if lasagna night falls on a Sunday so I can get things ready ahead of time."

I can't believe Dillie would rearrange her schedule to come eat lasagna with my family. I mean, it *is* her favorite food, but . . .

"I will," I say. "Thanks again for the coffee. I'll have to take my sister when she visits."

"Oh, no problem," Dillie replies. My mom waves to Dillie and tells her to have a good night, that she'll see me when I get inside. It's just the two of us again.

"See you later?" she says. The mysterious change in the air is back. She rests her head on the steering wheel, facing me.

"Yeah. Well, I guess I'll be hearing you later." There's a small voice in my head that wants to tell me how corny "hearing you later" is, but I quickly stomp it out.

"I won't hold you up from dinner," she says. "I think my mom is doing the usual tonight—roast beef and corn bread. Every Sunday, six p.m. on the dot."

"Sounds good, though," I say, taking off my seat belt, opening the door. "Have a good show—"

Then I hear it.

The song.

My song.

Where is it coming from? Dillie looks around for a second, thinking it's coming from her phone, until realization hits both of us.

It's coming from the radio.

My heart pounds as the familiar lyrics, familiar voice—my lyrics, my voice—come louder and louder through the speaker.

"Oh my gosh!" Dillie yells and claps. "It's the song! Listen to this version! It's super clear, too!" She turns the radio up.

It's true. This version wasn't the recorded, slightly muffled version that everyone was using for social media or playing in their cars. This is the mastered version, the one that only Dillie, Justin, Jerrod, and I have access to.

Something is up.

I need to figure out what.

But I can't let her know that I have anything to do with this. I can't be fazed.

Or I could use this chance to come clean. It'd be easy. Just tell her it's me, then sing the song, exactly as I'm singing it through the radio, right now. . . .

The thought seems less ridiculous than it did a month ago.

"How would *you* critique this singer?" Dillie suddenly asks, pointing to the radio.

"Huh?" My stomach flips. "Me?"

"Well, you already know my thoughts. But I'm biased. Remember how we talked about auto-tune and stuff? This singer isn't using auto-tune; his voice seems real. What do you think? Does mystery singer have the 'it' factor?" She gives me a lazy half smile, probably wondering what notes I have for this guy because I have notes for everyone else I hear.

She's asking me to critique myself.

"I—" What do I say? I listen to the lyrics, every riff, every harmony, every double we've added to this track. The way we've made it more layered. The stars of this song are the harmonies bouncing off the 808s.

I pretend that I'm not me, that I'm not the one expressing his love for Delia Dawson on the radio right now. Surprisingly, I like what I hear. It's not perfect. I played it safe vocally. I didn't try any daring notes.

But the song is honest. I meant every word. I felt alive while doing it. There are ways I could've made it better, but . . .

I sound great.

Dillie is still looking at me, waiting on my answer.

"He can sing," I finally say. "He has a lot of potential. It just depends on whether or not he decides to use it."

19: Record Scratch

When Dillie drives away and I walk into the house, I'm greeted by Justin, Mom, and Dad in the living room, and they all have the smiles of conspirators on their faces.

"Hey?" I say, raising my eyebrow at them.

"So, Dillie has you drinking coffee, huh?" Justin asks, waggling his own eyebrows, as if he wasn't there when the exchange actually happened.

"Yeah. We went to Nonna's. It was pretty good. Is dinner ready, Dad? I'm kind of hungry." I don't want to say much. The moment is still fresh, with just me and Dillie knowing the true details. I don't want all their opinions, especially before I've even had a chance to unpack my own.

"Oh, yeah. It's a new recipe, too. A casserole. Y'all let me know how it is. Be honest."

The three of us walk over to the dining room table and sit, while my dad goes into the kitchen and comes back out with a casserole. It looks and smells good. My stomach rumbles. We say grace and one by one, everyone takes a bite.

Dad is looking at all of us with a big grin, but it slowly disappears after the comments that follow.

"It's a little salty, Wyatt."

"The bottom is a little burned," I say. "But I mean, the sauce is really tasty, Dad," I apologetically add after seeing his frown. I know firsthand how critique can hurt.

"This isn't your best, Mr. Armstrong."

Dad throws his napkin down. "Well, shoot! Tell me how you really feel!"

"It's not bad, baby," Mama says. "It's just . . . it needs a little more love, that's all."

I disagree. It *is* bad. But I don't say this.

Dad sighs. "I've been trying to get this recipe right all week." I feel a little sorry for him. He was excited about the prospect of us loving his casserole.

"I don't know. It needs more than a little love," Justin says, jokingly. Justin has been my friend long enough for my family to have gotten used to his brutal honesty.

"Well, I'd like to see *you* try and make it," Dad huffs. "It's always the people sitting on the sidelines with the most to say."

I laugh at that, then stop. Am I on the sidelines?

"Touché," Justin says.

"At least you tried, Dad," I offer.

"Yeah, it's not the first nasty dish I'll make and it won't be the last," Dad admits. "We can just order pizza. I'll pack the casserole up and see if anyone at work wants it before I just get rid of it."

Mom and I make eye contact at this, but we wordlessly agree to let Dad's coworkers decide whether they think it is disgusting.

"So, Darren," my mom says, as my dad gets out his phone to order pizza. "You and Delia went on a coffee date?"

"It wasn't a coffee date," I say. Or was it? "She just took me there to try her favorite coffee after I took her to Sally's." The sooner I answer their questions, the sooner we can change the subject. I hope.

"Sounds like a coffee date to me," my dad says, not looking up from his phone. "Are y'all—what do the kids say these days—an *item*?"

I don't know about other kids, but none of my crew calls it "an item." "No, Dad," I say. "We're just . . . friends."

I sound cryptic, but that's exactly what it feels like. And then, there was that shift in the air earlier. The lingering looks, the softer, lower registers we were using for our voices . . .

"Did you tell her about the song?" Justin asks. He tries to whisper but considering there are only four of us at the table and they're all within earshot, everyone hears him.

"What song?" my mom asks. "Oh, for the contest, right?" Of course, she remembers.

"He wrote—"

"I wrote a song," I cut in, eyeing Justin, tired of him intervening on my behalf. I need to get ahead of my own story. "I wrote a song for Dillie. For fun. For her contest. I sent it anonymously, but it's getting popular, and it won, and she wants to know who's behind it." There. That's it.

"Speaking of the song, I heard the new version on the radio," I mutter to Justin, but everyone eyes me because, again, four people at the table. "You wouldn't know anything about that, would you?"

"Oh yeah! I had Jerrod pull some strings, and we sent it in."

"You *what*?" How does Justin even have the time to do all this meddling?

"Thank me later, bro." He says it like he's done me a favor, but I'm not so sure. It's like giving someone a big birthday gift that they didn't really ask for or want, but it was expensive so you don't say all of that.

My mom's eyes crinkle at the corners. She looks at me the way she looks when I tell her I made all As on my report card.

"Yes, Mama?" I ask, despite feeling exasperated. Why would Justin do that?

"You submitted a song anonymously and it won a contest. Sounds like true talent to me."

"Oh." I thought she was going to say something else about my crush on Dillie, but she's focused on the song instead.

"My baby. You were always a great singer."

"Mama . . ." I start, getting uncomfortable. She's acting like I won a Grammy or something.

"Well, when are you going to tell her you wrote the song?"

Dad asks, now looking up from his phone. "You are going to tell her. Right?"

Justin shakes his head at me before he takes another bite of casserole. He frowns at his plate.

"I don't know. There's no point now that we're . . ." I trail off. I don't say what I mean. There's no point if we're already hanging out. That was the point of the song.

Right?

"Son. I think there's a point. You just might be missing it." Dad gestures to the center of the table. "That casserole was nasty, but at least I'll make another one. You? You made a perfect meal, and you aren't taking credit for it. You're not even owning up to being a chef."

I stare at him. Is this about food? Or—

"Eventually the food will get eaten, or become stale, but I'll still be a chef. When this song dies down and nobody knows who sung it, will you still be a singer? Will you want to be?"

He taps a few buttons on his phone.

"Now are we doing pan pizza, or hand tossed?"

Later that night, after we had pan pizza and Justin went home, after I watch TV with my parents, then go upstairs to listen to Dillie's podcast, I lie in bed and think about what my dad said.

It's funny that life lessons surrounding Dillie tend to revolve around food. Especially since she's a self-proclaimed foodie. She shouts me out at the end of her podcast.

"This week, I had the best burger in town. I don't want to tell you about the place because it's a secret. But just know that it was better than Andy's Burger Joint."

I smile at this. I know she liked the burger, but I wonder if she liked the company she had while trying it?

"I agree. Let's keep Sally's a secret," I text her. I don't even have to think about it. It's an easy response, a great way to start this conversation.

I wait a full minute before I see the bubble on the screen, letting me know she's texting back.

Dillie: I knew you'd like it ☺ Who else knows about it?
Darren: Justin, his girlfriend Tiffany, his cousin Jerrod. That's it.
Dillie: Tiffany? They are back together?
Darren: Yup.

At least, I think so—who knows what could've happened in the last hour or so.

I shift a little in bed, getting comfortable as I tell her what I liked about this episode. I love texting for this reason—I have ample time to think about what I want to say, give a thoughtful answer to what *she* says. Her commentary on our school's football team and how she thinks they are going to go undefeated this year (which I agree with), some brand-new makeup she likes, new books she's reading or thinking about reading, her new favorite music. The homecoming dance.

Homecoming is coming up, so fast I almost forgot about it. It's almost a nonfactor—it's usually overshadowed by prom— but since the football team is doing so well this year, and most juniors at our school don't go to prom, there has been more buzz about going than usual.

As soon as she mentioned the dance, a thought popped in my head—*ask her*. If I could do that, then there was no need to *ever* mention the song.

But then it's like what my dad said. Would I still be a singer after the song dies down? Would I want to be? I could always start fresh, with a new song, but it seems like all that progress I made with "Dillie's Song" would be for nothing.

But it wouldn't, because I wrote that song for Dillie . . . even though she didn't like it.

If I didn't write it to show her how I felt . . . what did I write it for?

Who did I write it for?

The answer becomes clear in my mind.

I wrote it for me. A way to catch my thoughts and let them go.

I shake my head and look down at my phone, wondering again if I should ask Dillie to the dance.

This is it. The moment. If she says no, then she probably wouldn't want to go on any other dates either. Sally's, Nonna's, those were fun, casual. But the homecoming dance? This would be . . . official.

I take a deep breath, then type:

Darren: Do you have a date to the dance yet?

A text bubble forms, then stops, then forms again, letting me know that Dillie is typing, thinking. I keep trying to distract myself, humming song lyrics, scrolling mindlessly through emails, but my stomach dances knowing I'm waiting on her response. It takes so long, my screen goes black. Finally, I get a notification that she texted back. If she says no, I'll ask her to go with me. If she says yes, well, I guess that's that.

My finger hovers over the notification. Whatever she says could change everything. Finally, I click on it.

Dillie: Why?

Why?

I furrow my brow. I was prepared for a yes or no, but not a why. What does why mean?

"Why?" she asked with a scoff.

"I was . . . just wondering if you'd like to go with me."

"You thought I'd want to go with you just because we hung out a few times? You can't even come clean about really being the mystery singer."

I shake the daydream out of my head. We've been getting to know each other as friends . . . maybe it's too early to ask her on a real date. I don't want to ruin everything.

Darren: No reason.

I send this and instantly regret it. I don't have a feeling of peace, like I did when I didn't send the Clip comment or ask her out the day Justin gave his chicken sandwich analogy. Immediately, it feels like I blew it.

Suddenly, I get the feeling I got at Nonna's, when I told Dillie my passion was painting pictures, or at the open mic night, when I sung with an air of defeat. It almost feels like I'm doing this to myself on purpose.

I wait. The text bubble that lets me know she's typing disappears and appears again, twice.

Dillie: oh. Ok

My stomach drops. Me and my overthinking, me and my Delia Daydreams, have ruined the perfect chance to ask Dillie to the homecoming dance. If I ask her now, it will look like I'm doubling back.

I wake up the next morning in a haze. I love this part of the morning—where the dreams seem real and reality seems like a dream. Nobody expects anything from me. I can imagine a perfect world. But then I remember what happened last night. That I fumbled my chance to actually ask Dillie out on a date.

I check my phone and find a message from Justin, and the confusion hits me so hard I'm wondering if this is all just one big nightmare.

20: "Ain't Nothing Like the Real Thing, Baby"

I realize that while falling asleep (and texting Dillie), I missed a series of text messages from Justin:

Justin: That little taste of casserole made my stomach hurt. Tell your dad he should invite me over for the do-over to make up for it.
Justin: Tiffany and I are Off Again man. I gotta tell you about it.
Justin: You asked Dillie to the dance?! Proud of you, bro!

The last text stops me in my scroll, my thumb hovering over the message. I *didn't* ask Dillie to the dance. That, I know for sure.

But I check Dillie's text thread to make sure I didn't. I'm hit with the last few messages we've exchanged, and an air of sadness comes over me.

Where was Justin getting his information from?

I go back to his text thread, but too many developments happened overnight. I call him.

His phone rings a full four times before he answers. There's a shuffle of movement before he speaks.

"Bro, do you know what time it is?" he asks me. "It's—"

"Why did you say I asked Dillie to the homecoming dance?" I ask, hurriedly.

"It's on eClips," he mumbles into the phone. "She went live last night and said the mystery singer was going to reveal himself to her at the dance."

The mystery singer?

What's going on?

My thoughts swirl, none of them making sense.

I fill Justin in briefly on the happenings of last night—the texting, the homecoming dance . . .

"Oh, wow, Darren, you really messed up. So . . . it wasn't you that said that? Who was it, then?" Justin asks, sounding more awake now.

"I—I don't know. Look, I'll talk to you at school." We hang up and I instantly get on eClips to see the LiveClip Justin was talking about.

"Interesting developments happened in the last hour or so!" Dillie says as a few comments float by, asking her if she is going to the homecoming dance with anyone. I check the time stamp of the LiveClip, and it seems to be an hour or so after I fell asleep. After we ended our horrid conversation.

"Well . . . to be honest, I thought I was going with someone but . . ." She waves her hand in a motion, the same someone would use to shoo a mosquito away from their face. "I was wrong. But a few minutes later, get this—the mystery singer said he would reveal himself to me at the dance!"

I look at the eClip, my heart beating faster. What is happening?

Dillie laughs as a bunch of hearts and smiley faces float across the screen. "I know! It's a Cinderella moment waiting to happen! Finally, we will get to see who this mystery singer is, once and for all."

But how? How can she be going to the dance with the mystery singer when I'm the mystery singer and I ruined my chance to ask her?

"Does anyone have any guesses as to who you think it is?" she asks, as if she's reading my mind. But she isn't. This video is from the past.

Suddenly, Miles, the guy who "stole" my chorus solo, sends a bunch of wink faces across the screen, prompting another commenter to say, "I kind of have a feeling it's Miles!"

I roll my eyes. Why take credit for something you didn't even do?

Dillie smirks and says, "I guess we'll all find out soon enough." The LiveClip ends. My screen goes black and I see my face, confused with coal in my eyes.

I need to fix this.

As I turn into the parking lot of school, "Dillie's Song" plays on the radio.

I groan and rest my head on the steering wheel after I park

the car. I listen for a second to see if the DJ will announce who they think is singing it.

"This song has been highly requested this weekend by high schoolers," the DJ says. "It's funny because the singer doesn't have a name. Nothing even comes up when you try to search for it. I wonder if they'll reveal themselves soon."

I turn the car off and walk through the breezeway, to the atrium.

The hallways are crowded, the usual buzz of people talking and catching up before class is around me. I wonder how many people are talking about the mystery singer.

I almost bump into Tiffany. I tell her what's up, but she sneers and scoots past me. "Oh, shoot," I say to myself. I remember Justin saying they were Off Again. I try to find him so I can ask him about it, but I don't see him. He's not at his locker yet. Dang, we have so much we need to catch up on.

I walk to my own locker and wonder if I'll see Dillie there. I hope I do. Then, I make the sharp right turn down the hall and decide to walk to *her* locker this time instead.

She's standing there, just closing it and organizing the books in her hand. She looks up.

"Hey," she says, casually.

"Hey," I say, the coffee date and conversation from last night rushing back to me. In hindsight, it was the perfect lead-up to ask her to the dance and I just . . . didn't. What was I waiting on? Now it's too late.

I take a deep breath. "Look, about last night—" I start.

She does the mosquito hand motion again. "No worries. Really. We don't have to talk about it."

But I want to. I think. What should I even say?

"I . . ." This isn't the perfect moment. Should I still do it anyway? Isn't waiting for the perfect moment how I got into this mess in the first place?

"Dillie, I did want to ask you to the dance," I start, fighting against my nerves. "I just . . . I didn't know if you wanted to go with me."

Dillie scoffs. "Well, the only way that you would know is to ask me. And you didn't. What happened to stepping forward?" she says, referencing our conversation at Nonna's.

It stings. We literally talked about how the only way of knowing something is right or wrong is doing it. It was like a pop quiz on that same subject and I failed it.

"Plus, how do I know that you just aren't asking me now because you know that someone else wants to go with me?" she continues.

I raise my eyebrows. "No! No, that's not it at all. I mean, I know that you're going with the mystery singer, but—"

"Well, actually, we aren't *going* to the dance together." Her brow furrows as she thinks out loud. "He emailed me and told me he will reveal himself to me there. But still!"

"I—I thought you didn't know if the mystery singer was being truthful because he doesn't know you?" I ask, grasping at straws. This is ridiculous. How am I competing with myself for the same date?

"You're right. I don't know him, and he doesn't know me, but there's only one way to find out." She shrugs. "By *doing* it. It's just a dance. It'll either be fun or it won't. At least I'll still look nice and it will make for a great podcast episode either way."

I take a deep breath. "Dillie, I—"

The bell rings as if on cue.

Dillie sucks her teeth. "I gotta go. Mrs. Jones says if I'm late to her class again, I'll get detention." She starts to jog away. "I'll see you . . . around."

I sigh, filled with the extreme urge to bang my head against one of these lockers.

I watch her as she passes Justin's locker, when I realize I still haven't seen him.

Did he come to school today?

I pull out my phone and send a quick text in my locker, asking him if he was cutting class, then head to first period.

I sit in first block, putting my notebook on the desk, thinking about Dillie. How I messed up. How I need to tell her the truth.

The rest of the class pours in around me. Our teacher hasn't walked in yet. Figures. She always rushes in late and flustered, with a cup of coffee from the place my sister likes to go. I wonder distractedly if she's ever tried Nonna's.

"Aye, man," one of my classmates, Trey, says to me by way of greeting. I look up and nod at him as he takes his seat beside me.

"What's up?" I didn't think he was going to say anything back, but he follows up with, "Yo, you with Dillie now?"

He's not loud, but a few people look up at me.

I think about yesterday at the coffee shop, when I started to feel that connection between me and Dillie. Maybe if he asked yesterday, my answer would've been different. But not now.

I'm about to say no when I hear someone suck their teeth.

"Yeah, right. Him and Dillie ain't together, man."

Miles. He scoffs and makes a face as if to say "What a joke," and takes his seat. I raise my eyebrow. Yeah, I'm pretty quiet, but things change a little when someone insults me in front of my face. What's he getting at?

"I saw y'all in the hallway just now," Trey says, glancing at Miles and back to me. "I was just wondering. Maybe you were the mystery singer or something."

"We're just . . ." I'm about to say friends, but I trail off and shrug. I hope it doesn't give the impression that I don't care.

"Exactly. Nothing," Miles says, not looking up from his notebook, and laughs.

Trey glances at Miles again and back at me, a confused look on his face. I bet we're both thinking the same thing. *What's his problem?*

Then I realize. If Miles is supposedly taking credit for my

song, that means he must like Dillie, too. That's what the whole song is about.

"Did y'all hear that Dillie found the mystery singer on her podcast?" a girl named Morgan says. Her voice is high-pitched and squeaky, and everyone turns to her. "She posted on eClips last night."

At this, Miles smirks and leans back, licks his lips. Doing everything he can to make sure people look at him, which they do. I furrow my brow. Is he serious? I make to text Justin about it, then realize he didn't respond to my other message yet.

"Yeah, I did hear that," says another guy, Fred, who looks at Miles as if to challenge him. "Who knows," he says, leaning back. "It could be me."

Is this *real*? Are they really going to pretend like they made the song? Is Dillie going to have a bunch of suitors auditioning to fit the part of the mystery singer at the school dance?

Another girl, Tiana, turns around in her seat and looks at us. "She says she's going to finally meet him at the dance!"

People say various names among themselves, and not one of them suspects me.

"I heard it's her ex. He's trying to get back with her and she's going to go for it," a girl named Melanie says. "That's why she hasn't announced it yet. I mean, the entire show started because he broke up with her in the first place. She used it to get him back and he didn't want to get back together." She shakes her head. "It'd look embarrassing to go back to him now."

I sneer at this guess. Back with her *ex*? I didn't even consider that. What if this propels him to reach back out, and they start dating?

But then I think back to what she said yesterday at Nonna's: *I'd never want him back.*

And I remember how she said that people thought she was trying to get back with her ex through her show and how that wasn't true. I look at Melanie. She's sitting at her desk, with a look of contempt, like she's just dropped some hard-hitting facts.

"She's not back with her ex," I can't help but say. I don't like the fact that Melanie is making the show all about Dillie's ex-boyfriend. I mean, has Melanie even bothered to listen to it?

I look around, at Miles, Melanie, and Fred. At the ease that people can make up their own stories.

"Well, who is it then?" she challenges.

"Well, isn't it obvious?" Miles pipes in loudly.

Everyone turns to look at him.

"Is it?" I ask. Then everyone turns to look at me. I don't say a lot in class, but I think everyone can pick up on the tension between the two of us.

"Yeah," Miles says, turning all the way around in his seat to face me. "I think it is."

"You know, it does sound like . . ." Morgan slowly points to Miles. A few other girls look at each other and nod, then glance at Miles again. He nods, a smug look on his face.

My heart beats a little faster. Sure, I may have blown my chances with Dillie, but whoever claims to be the mystery singer was also claiming my song. And even if Dillie doesn't think the mystery singer meant those words, I do. It was fine when no one was taking credit, when the song was finally starting to die down, when it was a way to express how I felt about Dillie. But it's more. It's *my* song.

It reminds me, again, of my mom. *Hard work beats talent when talent doesn't work hard*. I think, finally, it's okay to admit that I have talent. And that I'm not working hard enough on it.

I may not be a big talker or a bragger, but without a doubt, I've always had a voice. And that's my upper hand here.

I weigh my options. I can't say it's me now. Not before I tell Dillie. No one would believe me.

So I say nothing.

My silence speaks loudly, because suddenly everyone discussing Dillie looks at me.

"You're trying to see who's after your girlfriend?" Trey asks me. I realize that's probably what some people in here are thinking. Morgan and Tiana whisper something to each other and look at me, too.

Still, I say nothing.

Everybody is making their move, except for me, and now it's my turn.

But not yet.

I am not procrastinating out of fear, but nobody in here needs to know what I'm about to do.

The only two people I need to talk to right now are Dillie and Mrs. Thompson.

It's time to take matters into my own hands.

At that moment, the teacher finally walks in, balancing her coffee, bag, a few books, and a water bottle. She's probably as flustered as I feel.

I'm tapping my pencil against my desk, even though I've already turned in my economics quiz.

A student aide knocks on the door with a blue slip excusing me from the end of class to see my guidance counselor. I speed walk to the small building. I'm just about to sit down in front of the fountain when Mrs. Thompson peeks her head from her office into the waiting room.

"Come on in, Darren," she says, waving me toward her office. I glance at the clock before I follow her. Ten minutes before lunch. I thought about waiting, but Mrs. Thompson is out the rest of the week, and if I wait too long, I might not be able to make the schedule change. I have to do this. I want to do this.

"Darren, it's so nice to see you again so soon," she says, sitting down behind her desk, already typing. I sink down into the same cushy armchair I did before.

She types a little more and looks up at me with a proud look on her face. "So, you want to rejoin the school chorus?"

I nod.

I know this doesn't seem directly related to Dillie, but the whole situation made me realize that even if it doesn't ever work out with us, I don't want to lose the other thing I really care about: music.

"Good news. Normally Mr. Drummond wouldn't allow students to join school chorus this late unless they're transfers. But since it's you, he couldn't have been more thrilled to hear you wanted to come back. You'll only have to re-audition for your spot as the section leader."

"Okay." I nod, smiling at Mrs. Thompson. I can almost feel the crisp sheet music in my hands, the old-but-reliable piano Mr. Drummond plays as we sing. I didn't realize how much I missed it.

"Thanks, Mrs. Thompson," I say. "Really." Now I can drop that boring study hall period for good.

"Darren, it's no problem," she says, right as the lunch bell rings. "I'm happy you decided to add something you love back into your schedule. See you soon."

I wave at her and turn to walk out her office when I see it again. The photograph of the woman holding the microphone.

"Mrs. Thompson, I'm sorry but I have to ask again," I say. "Is this you?"

She nods excitedly. "Yes, it is. Many, many moons ago."

"You were a famous singer?" I know I'm being nosy, but I can't help it.

"I don't know if famous is the right word, but I did sing professionally."

I wonder what happened. Did she quit? Get booed off the stage? Lose a record deal? How did she end up being a guidance counselor? "Why did you stop?" I ask.

"I never stopped singing. Me and some of my girlfriends run a small ensemble and we sing around the city. You might see us Christmas caroling this year. I love this much better. And I love helping kids figure out their dreams, too."

"Oh," I say. "That's actually kind of cool."

"Thank you. I have no regrets. I don't want you kids to have any either."

"Thanks again, Mrs. Thompson."

She winks at me. "Us singers have to stick together."

21: CacoPHONY

Now that I am officially back on the school chorus, I feel excited. Maybe I can audition to get my solo back. I hum songs in math class and through a test, until my teacher finally shushes me.

I'm still in a fairly good mood on my way to Justin's house, until I hear "Dillie's Song" on the radio *again*. It makes me wonder who is trying to take credit. I chew over in my mind how to handle this. I'll talk it over with Justin. I figure he's sick or something. He still hasn't responded to any of my texts, and I didn't see him at school.

His car is there when I pull into Justin's driveway.

I knock on the door. It reminds me of when we were kids, before we had cell phones, and we could only walk to each other's houses to see if the other was available to play.

I wait awhile before I knock again. I'm wondering if he's taking a nap when the door creaks open.

"What's up, bro," he says hoarsely, giving me a weak smile.

Now, my mama always told me it's rude to tell people they look sick or tired, but Justin definitely looks like he's had a rough day. He's in what I'm assuming are pajamas—old, ratty plaid pants and a wrinkled, stained white T-shirt. He has bags under his swollen eyes.

"Uh . . . you good, bro?" is all I can say.

Justin sighs, a long one that takes away his fake smile and slumps his shoulders. "No. I gotta tell you about it." He turns around and walks upstairs to his room.

I sit in Justin's designated gaming chair while he plops onto his own bed and sighs again. "Tiffany broke up with me. For good."

I don't say anything at first. Justin's said these exact words to me before approximately one hundred fifty times. Every time I try to give the same reactions. "Aw, man, for real?" I start.

"For real this time, man, seriously," he says, rubbing his temples. "I *know* she was serious this time."

"What makes this time so different?" I ask.

He just shakes his head. "I can just tell."

He does seem sadder than normal. Usually, when Justin and Tiffany are Off Again, it just means another weekend of us going to parties where Tiffany and Justin look at each other the entire night but pretend not to. It never meant staying home from school.

"I'm sorry to hear that, man." I can't tell whether he wants advice or condolences yet, so I just leave it at that.

"Yeah. Thanks," he says. Then, "Did I miss anything at school today?"

I'm not ready to talk about school chorus yet. I want to keep it a secret for just a little while longer. Everyone will find out soon enough.

"Umm . . . I saw Tiffany today, but she just mean-mugged me."
He gives a halfhearted shrug.

"Oh, tell me why Miles tried to play me today in class."

"What?"

I tell him the story, and what happened when I saw Dillie today.

"Yo, he is such a weirdo. And I'm sorry about Dillie. I would say I told you so, but I don't even feel like it. What are you going to do when the fake mystery singer shows up at the dance?"

I shrug. "I don't know. I thought about not going, but that won't stop any of this. I feel like even if I do tell Dillie it's me now, she won't want to hear it."

"Hmm," Justin says, thinking. I wait for his suggestions on exactly how to execute this, but none comes. Wow, Justin must be in worse shape than I thought. He never passes up a chance to give his opinion.

"So, what did she say about the email? Did she seem excited about meeting the mystery singer?"

"She said—"

Wait a minute.

"What did you say?" I ask.

"I said, what did Dillie say about the email—I mean, uh, what the mystery singer said?" His eyes shift.

I didn't mention the email. As a matter of fact, I forgot to.

"Justin, how did you know the mystery singer sent Dillie an email?" I ask.

"I just assumed that whoever told her had to do it through

email, since it was a secret." He shifts his eyes again. "How else would they tell her? Right?"

I think about this.

"Be honest with me," I say. "Justin, are you the person who emailed Dillie saying the mystery singer would meet her at the dance?"

Justin scrunches up his face and looks at me incredulously, then sighs, as if it's too much.

"Yeah."

I raise my eyebrows. "Why?"

Justin sighs again, but it just turns into a loud groan. "*Because*, man! We're friends. You had everything you've ever talked about in your grasp, and you were willing to give it up! I don't think you know how big that song is right now. I've heard people driving by bumping it at least five times today. You were gonna pass it up and let everyone think Miles or Dillie's ex-boyfriend, or whoever, wrote it, and try to get what's supposed to be yours. Except they can't because it's *yours*, so the song just goes to waste. You think that the song doesn't matter anymore because she doesn't like it, but it's more than that. You chose to express yourself in song for a reason because you love singing. I just wanted you to realize that."

I frown. Justin doesn't know that I'm already thinking the same way he does. But I hate that he went ahead of me to do something without asking, without letting me come to my own conclusion about it first.

First, Jerrod sent Dillie the song, then Justin sent it to the radio station, and then Justin told Dillie that I was ready to reveal my identity. Why can't *anything* about this song happen on my own terms?

"You really wanna know why Tiffany and I broke up?" Justin continues before I can respond. "Because when I sent the email, Tiffany caught me and thought *I* was the mystery singer. Me! And I couldn't deny it because she saw the email and—"

"And telling her the truth would mean telling her about me," I finish.

Justin nods.

My stomach twists a little bit. Maybe it's the nuggets I had for lunch, but I feel a little guilty about what happened. He was just trying to help.

But . . . I'm also mad at him. Just like I ruined it for myself by chickening out of asking Dillie to the dance, Justin ruined it for himself by meddling.

"Justin, you always do this!" I burst out. "And I'm tired of it. I'm tired of everyone trying to make me do what they feel like I should do, when *they* feel like I should do it. This time, *you* did too much and now you messed up your own relationship. I don't need your help right now, man. I got this."

Justin frowns at me.

"You *got* this? Bro, the entire reason I did this was because you weren't going to! I was trying to help."

"How do you know what I was going to do?" I ask. "I spent

more time with Dillie after you and Jerrod pushed me to the first time, by myself."

Why am I being so mean? Justin is clearly hurt, and I don't want to make things worse. I stand up, getting ready to leave.

Justin must take this as a threat, mistaking it for a fighting stance, because he stands up too.

"Without Jerrod sending the song in the first place, none of this would be happening! I sent that song to the radio station because you were sad that nobody liked it. I thought if you heard it on the radio, you'd feel motivated to tell her and you *still* didn't!

"Darren, we've been friends for years, and I've watched you live your whole life in your head. It's one thing to dream or—or think about things you're excited about. But the things you're dreaming about are happening right in front of you and you were just letting them. Don't you want the real experiences, too?"

Too much is happening today, and I don't feel in control of any of it. I just need time to think, to process what's going on. "Right now, I just want you to stay out of it."

It came out a lot harsher than I meant it to, but I can't take it back. Justin looks surprised at first, then angry. Finally, he shrugs.

"Fine, leave. Stay in your head, then."

I walk out of his room and down the stairs. More and more, I'm feeling like living outside of my daydreams is not worth the trouble.

22: Mama Knows Best

I walk in the door with the intention of going to my room and replaying the past two days in ways that I would have rather they'd gone, when I see my mom sitting on the couch, reading a book.

"Oh, hey, Darren," she says. "Your dad is catering—why the long face?"

Oh no. If I don't look at her, maybe she won't be able to get the truth out of me with those round eyes.

"Darren? Look at me," she says.

Well, maybe not.

I look at her and instantly she gets off the couch and walks over to me. "Tell me what's wrong."

I rub a hand over my face. I was mean to Justin and messed up with Dillie. I definitely don't want to say the wrong thing to my mom.

I don't know, I'm just tired of feeling misunderstood.

"Misunderstood about what?" she asks.

Wait. Did I say that out loud?

"Um. That's not what I meant to say."

"Are you sure?"

"Ummm . . ."

"Let's sit down."

When I was little, every so often Mama would pick me up from school early and we'd go to my favorite fast-food place and drink milkshakes in the car. Just the two of us. I'm sure she had her own thing going on with Zoe, too, but I loved that alone time.

It feels just like one of those days when I sit on the couch, sigh, and try again. "I got into an argument with Justin and I blew things with Dillie this week. Justin keeps overstepping even though I know he's only trying to help. And with Dillie . . . I was so focused on waiting until the right moment to ask her out that I missed my chance completely."

She just nods and motions for me to keep going.

"Maybe it wouldn't have been too late, but Justin messed it up by trying to help. He thinks that I won't and can't do anything without his meddling, but that's not true."

"Why is that not true?" she asks.

"Because I'm . . . um . . ."

"Go on," she encourages.

"I can sing. I'm a good listener, at least most of the time. I'm intentional. I have a good musical ear . . . or so I thought. Even if sometimes it takes me a while to do something. I guess I'm just afraid of messing up, like I did these past two days."

"Baby, you're going to make mistakes," Mama says. "Shoot, we all do. The important thing is to keep going."

"I know, but now I just feel like I learned my lesson too late to 'keep going.'" I sigh. "And I was just getting over the whole open mic thing and the whole world booing me."

"The world? Are you sure? The world is pretty big." My mom laughs. "It sounds like you care too much about what people think. Well, I guess we all do, especially at your age. Your friends know you. Maybe the world doesn't, but maybe it doesn't need to. That's a whole lotta people to please."

I smile. I will keep this advice close as people inevitably don't like my music or singing in the future.

"As far as Dillie goes, did you do something really terrible? If not, maybe there is still a chance. But give it your *all*. That way, at least you'll know that you tried your very best and you can move on peacefully."

I nod. "I think that was my issue with open mic night. I couldn't move on because I know I didn't try my very best."

"You feel like you gave up before you even got started?"

I nod again. With singing and with Dillie.

I give my mama a hug. "Thanks, Mama," I say. "I needed this little talk." I stand up to go to my room. Maybe instead of replaying what I did wrong today, I can think about what I can do right tomorrow.

"Anytime, baby. Oh, and can you get something out of the freezer for me? You'll know it when you see it."

I walk to the kitchen and open the freezer and see two milk-shakes. Just like old times. I laugh out loud.

"Mama? Really?"

She walks into the kitchen and squeezes my shoulder.

"Darren, mamas just know."

23: Studio Session

"All right. You ready?" Jack asks.

I nod, my hand on my headphones. Jerrod is here since the beat is his.

We've been at the studio for about an hour, working on a song that's been forming in my head these past few weeks. Jerrod helped a little with the structure, and once we set it to one of his beats, I changed a few words here and there to really make it fit.

The first song I wrote was for Justin and Jerrod. The mastered version of that song was for Dillie. But this song is for me.

As I put on my headphones, I remember one of the reasons why I love to sing: to feel understood. But now I'm realizing it's not so others can understand me; it's so I can understand myself.

"Yeah. I'm ready."

The new beat is the same type of vibe as the slower version of "Dillie's Song." Now the song is complete and I'm in the studio, about to start recording it for the first time.

"My thoughts are a steady rhythm of you . . ."

It finally feels right.

I'm just about to leave the studio when the door swings open. In walks Justin.

"What are you doing here?" we both say to each other.

"I called both of you to hash things out." Jerrod grins proudly, showing today's shiny gold grill on his teeth.

I shake my head. This family *cannot* help but meddle.

Although, I do want to clear the air. I'm ready to move past this entire thing. I understand that Justin has been wanting to help me. I just needed to set boundaries on how he does. Plus, I was a bad friend. Too in my own head to help him with his problems.

"Well? Go on. Hurry up, I have a party to go to after this," Jerrod says.

"Yeah, and you have about one hour left before your session is over and we haven't mastered this song yet," Jack chimes in.

I look at Justin. He still has on raggedy clothes, which is uncharacteristic for him. I take it he and Tiffany are still Off Again.

I guess since Jerrod facilitated this meeting, I'll be the one to start talking. "Look, I'm sorry for what I said. I didn't mean for you to 'stay out of it.' Well, I did, but I know you mean well."

Justin sucks his teeth. "It's not just that," he says. "You were so wrapped up in Darren's World, you weren't even seeing what's going on around you anymore! I've been trying to tell you for weeks that Tiffany and I were rocky. I help you with everything, but you can't even tell me if I was truly wrong for what I did last week! I'm literally on the phone with radio stations trying to send in your song but all you could say to me was 'I don't know.' You didn't even say anything about me and Tiffany breaking up, when I already told you that morning."

I vaguely recall Justin asking for my advice about Tiffany, but I was too distracted by all this commotion about the song to really pay attention.

I think back to the early morning text from the other day. I remember reading about him and Tiffany and skimming past it to the news about Dillie. Okay, I should feel guilty about that. The thing about living in my head is, my thoughts are the only ones that matter. But in the real world, I have real people to care about, too.

"My bad, man," I say.

Justin just shakes his head. "Yeah, I overstepped. But it's because I care. I couldn't let another year go by of you thinking about Dillie when she's right in front of you. Or think about what it would be like to sing again when you have a top song out right now. I didn't even *know* you sung like that, bro. You let that dream fade away in your head. But it's happening right now and . . . I wanted you to see it."

There's silence. A very awkward one. It's clear that Justin believes in me as a singer, as a potential boyfriend for Dillie, as a person. It's something I really appreciate. But . . .

"Justin, you are my friend, you're my brother, but stop trying to fix me," I say. "Yeah, I took a little bit longer to do what I want, but at least I got there. I like to think—I'm a thinker. But . . . it doesn't stop there. I need to be able to figure things out and mess up on my *own* and trust my own decision-making without you or anyone else doing it for me."

"I wasn't trying to fix you," Justin says. "Do you honestly think you would've gotten there without Jerrod's and my help?"

I pause to think about this. Would I? If Jerrod hadn't sent that song, Dillie probably would've never heard it. It never would've blown up around the city. I would've never recorded it officially. But I'm still in the studio, today, doing something totally different. I still rejoined school chorus.

"I would've still got there," I say. "But maybe I did need a little push from you and Jerrod at first. So . . . thank y'all. For real."

"That's what friends are for, man." He sighs. "Sorry. I'll back out of your business."

"It's all good. And we both know that isn't true, but you can back out of it at least a little bit."

We laugh and dap each other up. It's true. Justin and Jerrod and my parents and my sister all try to give their unsolicited advice, but I know they mean well. They just want to see me do my best. But I got it from here.

"So, you and Tiffany are still Off Again, huh?"

Justin frowns. "How do you know we're still Off Again?"

"Because you got on these funky clothes," I say.

Justin sighs. "Yeah, I've tried everything and I've got nothing left. I guess we are all loveless and dateless to the homecoming dance."

"Not *me*," Jerrod says. "Destiny and I are back good. We might go to y'all's homecoming dance, actually."

"How, when you have to be invited by someone that goes to our school?" Justin asks.

"I don't reveal my secrets," Jerrod says.

"Maybe we just go to the club that same night," Justin suggests.

Absolutely not.

But Justin gives me an idea.

He's tried everything, but I haven't.

I take a deep breath. The scale of an idea this big has only ever existed in my head. But the thought of trying it in real life was kind of exciting.

Maybe there is a way to give it my all, with Dillie and with my music.

"Not all is lost," I say. "I have an idea."

"Really?" Justin's eyes widen.

"Okay, y'all remember the movie *Cinderella*?"

Justin and Jerrod both respond with a blank stare.

"Just—go with it, okay? Dudes have been popping up left and right trying to say that they are the mystery singer and meeting Dillie at the dance, just like in *Cinderella*. All of those girls were lying and saying they had the glass slipper."

"Where are you going with this?" Justin asks.

"Okay, so I have the glass slipper."

"Which is?"

"The song, Justin! My singing! I am the only one who can sing that song. And I'm going to do it at the dance."

"Can I be the Icy Godbrother?" Jerrod says, flashing his gold grill.

Justin groans. "Darren, this metaphor is giving me a headache. What is your plan?"

"I'm going to email Dillie and tell her that the mystery singer won't be just revealing himself to her at the dance, but also serenading her. I do need y'all's help, though. Jerrod, you know DJ Scoop, right? I need him to get ready for a performance."

Justin rubs his chin and nods. "I like this idea, Darren. Especially as one I didn't have to come up with."

I smile. "Thanks, man. I mean, she may still not go for it, but at least I will try. Now let's fix *your* situation with Tiffany, since me and apparently Jerrod are going to the dance."

Justin grimaces. "Yeah, about that. I looked at Tiffany's eClips yesterday and it looks like Tiffany and Dillie are going to the dance together."

"What?" I say. "How?"

"Well, I guess since Tiffany and I are Off Again, she didn't have a date. Dillie doesn't technically have a date until she gets there, you know, to meet the mystery singer. Maybe she wants Tiffany to go with her in case things get awkward."

I groan. This definitely throws a wrench in the plan.

"Even if we do get back together, she won't want to leave Dillie hanging."

"We need to go as a group," I say, snapping my fingers. "That way, you can still go with Tiffany."

"Will Dillie want to go in a group with you?" Jerrod asks. "You know, since you played her and all."

"I didn't play her," I say. How does he even know this?

"If she's anything like Tiffany, she'll definitely want to go in a group so you can see what you're missing by not asking her out. Hmm, maybe Tiffany can suggest this."

"But you and Tiffany aren't On Again yet," I say. I rub my eyes. "Let's start with one thing at a time. Let me send this email."

Jerrod, Justin, and for some reason, Jack huddle around me as I log in to MysterySinger@ClipMail.com and send Dillie an email telling her that I will be serenading her in front of everyone at the homecoming dance.

With every word, I stop, hesitating. Do I really want to do this? But I force myself to keep going.

"It's done," I say when I hit send. Here goes nothing.

"What should we do about Tiffany?" I ask. "She only broke up with you because she thought you were the mystery singer, right?" Maybe a romantic gesture from Justin plus me telling her that I am the mystery singer can help smooth this over. "Can she keep a secret?"

Justin nods vigorously. "Yup. She never told anyone when . . . well, I can't tell you that."

"I don't want to know," I say. "But I have an idea. Let Jack master this track and we can put this plan in motion."

◆ ◆ ◆

"Play it one more time," I say, leaning back.

As the song plays, I picture myself singing it to Dillie, her smiling back at me in the audience. I showed off on the runs, and the harmonies, even more so than "Dillie's Song." I wanted it to sound like me, something I'm proud of.

I hold on to that vision. It may be another Dillie Daydream, but I'm working hard to make this one come to life.

The song finishes. The three guys in the room look at me.

"Well?"

"It's perfect."

After a few hours of running around town, buying huge custom balloons that barely fit into Justin's car, buying Tiffany's favorite ice cream, and me ensuring her that I am the real mystery singer and Justin has zero interest in Dillie, Justin and Tiffany are back On Again, and Tiffany, completely enamored with the romance of it all (and her new balloons), agreed to help us.

I lie on my bed and see a notification from eClips, from Dillie. She took a poll asking everyone to help her choose a homecoming dress.

@dillie_d: Which one do you like better? I can't decide.

They are both of Dillie, posing in a mirror, in where I can only guess is her room. I see a bed and desk in the background.

The two pictures load. In the first one, she's wearing a navy-blue top that wraps around her neck and has beads all over it. There's a skirt to match, and a slither of skin separating the two. I can see the beginning of the curve of her waist. She looks beautiful.

The second one though . . .

She's wearing a burgundy dress. The material is flowy and looks like it would continue to move around, even if she stops. She stands with her leg out, accentuating the slit in the dress going up to her thigh. The dress is low cut with thin straps, and she wears a gold choker around her neck. Her lipstick is the same color as the dress, making her lips seem more pouty, and fuller than usual.

I think of my closet and remember the burgundy tie my dad bought me for my birthday last year. I vote for that one, hoping by the end of the night we can be standing by each other, matching.

I'm exhausted, and nervous. I keep telling myself that even if this doesn't work to woo Dillie, I can at least focus on my music.

I keep telling myself that it's okay if no one likes it, or if I get booed, again.

I keep trying to convince myself not to quit.

Even if it's getting harder and harder to do that.

24: Crescendo

After another bland day at school, I pull into my driveway and am greeted by an unfamiliar gray car, parked where I usually do behind my parents. I'm annoyed, because I know my mom is going to ask me to come outside and move my car when whoever this is leaves.

My key is in the door, and I don't even get a chance to turn the lock before it opens.

"Baby bro!" I'm greeted by a freckle-faced girl with long, dark box braids down her back. My sister, Zoe.

"Oh, what's up, Z!" We hug. "I didn't know you were coming this early."

"Thanksgiving break starts earlier for us, and I'm exempted from some of my exams so I got to come even sooner."

"Of course you did. Hey, whose car is that?"

Her cheeks turn pink a little. "Darren, I have somebody I want you to meet."

We walk into the house, where my parents are sitting on the couch, across from a guy who looks about Zoe's age. He seems confident, unfazed by my dad's aggressively raised eyebrow—an expression I get from him. My mom is smiling conspiratorially, looking back and forth between them. She loves to watch my dad squirm over Zoe's boyfriends.

"Darren, this is Brandon. My—boyfriend."

She trips over the word, which doesn't matter because our parents are going to call whoever we bring to meet them our "little friends," probably until the day we get married.

He looks at me and I realize he's the full-bearded guy who butted in on our conversation that time. But Zoe is uncharacteristically fidgety, which means Dad already embarrassed her a little, so I keep my own eyebrow in place and dap him up. "What's up," I say. "Uh, y'all go to school together?"

She nods. "Brandon is premed."

"What kind of doctor will you be?"

"Dentist," he says.

Hm. Nice.

I was going to go up to my room and work on the idea Justin and I came up with, but it feels awkward to leave, so I sit on the sofa beside my parents.

"Darren, what have you been up to?" Zoe asks. She slides seamlessly onto the arm of the sofa next to Brandon. He offers her the entire chair, but she shakes her head.

"Zoe prefers the arm of that chair to anything else," I say to Brandon. I had to get my "I know my sister better than you" dig in.

I turn back to Zoe. "But, you know, the usual." I pause, then add, "I'm singing again." Instead of guessing or obsessing about what people think in my head, I let it roll off my back. And I'm realizing there is a surprise element—you never know what people are actually gonna say.

Zoe's eyes get wide. "Really? Darren, I'm so proud of you! Have you recorded anything yet?"

Dad makes a show of turning to look at me, wondering if I'm going to tell her.

I am. "You know that song—" I clear my throat and start to sing it, in front of everyone. Brandon leans back in surprise, and Zoe gasps, jumps up, and squeals.

"*Tell me* that's not you. Oh my gosh, you're *lying*!" Zoe yells. "That's your song? I should've known! How did I not know?"

"Wow, that's really dope, man," Brandon says easily. "You have a good voice. Are you going to record something else soon?"

"Record something else, and also tell the world that's you singing, right?" Zoe puts a hand on her hip. "I know you, Darren. I know you're going to try to keep this a secret forever—"

"I'm performing the song at our homecoming dance this weekend," I declare. The more I say it out loud, the less nervous I feel. In my mind, the words get wrapped up in doubt. Saying them out loud makes it all feel more real and easy.

"Homecoming dance?" my mom asks. "Are you going with Delia?"

"Delia?" Zoe looks back to me, to my parents, and back to me. "You're seeing Dillie?"

My mom looks at me to tell my story, her eyes big and bright, the same ones my sister is drilling into the side of my face.

"It's a long story," I say. "But no. Hopefully that will change after the dance."

Zoe processes this information. "I've been listening to her show . . ." she says thoughtfully. "Does she know you're the singer?"

I shake my head. "Not yet."

"Are you going to tell her before the performance?" she asks. Then gasps again, then looks at Brandon as if she has a new idea. "Oh! You could surprise her—"

"And let her find out during the performance?" I finish. "Yup, that's what I plan on doing."

Zoe folds her arms across her chest. "Hm. Okay. I see you, little bro."

I smile. "Thank you, Zo. What do y'all have planned for the rest of the night?"

"Well, we were going to have dinner and then Brandon was going to check into a hotel," my dad says, playfully.

Brandon laughs. "I was actually going to crash at a friend's tonight before I go to Charleston to visit my parents." Charleston was only a few hours' drive from here.

I smirk. "Zoe, were you going to go with him?"

Her head snaps toward me and I chuckle. I can guess she was planning on it, but hasn't talked about it with my parents yet.

"I know not for Thanksgiving, right?" My mom cocks her head to the side.

"No! No . . ." Zoe says. "I was just going to go and . . . meet his parents. Brandon was going to show me around his childhood neighborhood . . . that's all."

Her cheeks are beet red at this point.

We eat a dinner of tacos and nachos. Brandon ends up being cool and funny, Dad doesn't embarrass us too much. Then, Zoe and Brandon announce they're going to a movie before Brandon heads to his friend's house.

"Darren, I need you to move your car," my mom and Zoe say in unison.

I grab my keys. "I was going out anyway."

Everyone turns to me, but only Zoe, Mom, and Dad ask, "Where are you going?"

I hesitate for a second. "I'm going to the studio to work on a song." I feel bare and exposed. Singing is one thing, but creating is another, and I've already shared too much.

"Ooh." Zoe's eyes brighten. "About what?"

"I . . ." I stop. I can share more, but I don't have to tell them my entire plan.

"You'll know when it's ready."

I walk outside, making sure I have everything I need, including my legal pad, and make my way to the studio.

25: Countdown

Tonight's the night.

I'm in my room, brushing my hair and checking my suit one more time—Dillie confirmed on eClips that she is wearing the burgundy dress, so I'm wearing a suit with the burgundy tie, and some burgundy and cream argyle socks that show when I sit down. I got a fresh haircut this morning, and just took my do-rag off a few seconds ago, so my waves are perfect.

I check my phone, but no texts yet. The plan is officially in motion. Apparently, Dillie said that she didn't want to ruin Tiffany's night, so she can go to the dance with Justin since they are On Again. Tiffany told her that she definitely wouldn't leave her hanging for a guy (I am left wondering when they became friends), so they could still all go to the dance together . . . the caveat being that we are all meeting at my house. Dillie was skeptical about this at first, but once Tiffany told her that "it'll be fun to watch Darren squirm seeing you in that dress," Dillie was . . . cool with it.

I am already squirming for more reasons than one, so Tiffany called this correctly.

Dillie, Justin, and Tiffany are all meeting here around eight so we can go to the dance together.

We went over our plan last night, during halftime when Morgan Jackson, the squeaky-voiced girl from homeroom, was crowned homecoming queen. She's the first Black homecoming queen we've ever had at school, which is cool and sad at the same time. Dillie intends to have her on the show this week.

Next week's show will be dedicated to the mystery singer. The band played the song last night, and it took everything in me not to get up and start singing with them, especially since Miles got up and started pop-locking and doing all types of other dance moves, as the student body, including the cheerleaders, egged him on.

"One more day," Justin whispered to me, as even Tiffany started dancing beside him.

Now the doorbell rings, and I know it's Justin. The only person who would come to my house without telling me he's on the way.

"Darren!" my mom calls from downstairs. "The door is for you!"

I head down to find Justin and Tiffany standing in the foyer, talking to my parents. I see my mom ask Tiffany to give her a spin and she does. She's wearing a sparkly purple dress, and Justin is wearing a suit with a purple tie and, for some reason, sunglasses. Their outfits are flashy, but perfect for them.

"Okay, Darren! I see you!" Justin compliments me as I reach the last stair. We dap each other up, and I return the compliment and say hello to Tiffany.

"Ready for tonight?" she asks, smirking.

I nod, gulping. In the back of my mind, I know I could just . . . not do this. I try to shake it out of my head, but the thought almost seems comforting.

A small part of me starts to get nervous. Again. I shake it out and focus on the moment.

"Ooh, I can't wait to see what her pretty self is going to have on," my mom muses.

"You'll love it, Mom," I say, knowing it's true.

The dance starts at eight o'clock, but of course we don't want to arrive on time. But for our plan to work, I do want to arrive by nine.

We exchange polite banter for a few more minutes until I check my watch again. It's 8:00 p.m.

Where is she?

I check my social media. She posted a picture two hours ago (a picture of what looked like a nail salon) stating that she was getting ready, but nothing since.

I rub my hands against my pants. I daydream about going to the dance but not singing. Or maybe not even going.

Doubt creeps into my mind. I don't have to perform. I don't even have to *go* to this dance. Sure, Justin, Jerrod, and probably Tiffany would be upset, but I could make it up to them. I could lie in bed and think of a perfect scenario of tonight, without any mess-ups. And maybe I could still sing, pushing my songs anonymously . . .

"She should be here soon, right?" my dad asks, checking his

watch, pulling me back to reality. They are going out to dinner since Zoe and I will be out, but their reservation is for 8:15. I don't want them to leave without seeing her, but they might have to.

We take things out of the foyer and into the living room, as Justin asks for a glass of water to stall. (Thanks, Justin.)

At 8:20, we hear a car outside. My heart suddenly thumps in my chest, but I will myself to relax. It could just be Zoe.

But I take a second, then stand up and walk to the door. I open it, and my breath gets caught in my lungs.

It's Dillie, in the burgundy dress, wearing matching lipstick and a tiny gold choker around her neck. I register that this is my first time seeing her since she told me the mystery singer was meeting her at the dance. Her already curly hair is styled into even bigger curls, falling down the side of her face. Her skin is glowing; when she smiles her signature grin, a gold powder catches the light across her cheeks.

"Hi, Darren," she says, breathlessly. "I'm sorry I'm late—I had to make sure my little sister knew what her chores were before I left the house."

The second part was more for Tiffany, who comes over and hugs her.

"Dang, chores on a Saturday?" I say, trying to make conversation with her. Wanting her to look at me, to feel what I feel for her.

She does look at me, and her eyes linger. "She's grounded. Again," she says, and she starts talking to Tiffany again.

"Aw, man. I remember those days. I think I spent my entire

ninth-grade year being grounded for staying out too late with Justin."

I chuckle a little, trying to break the ice, but the conversation isn't flowing as smoothly as it has been lately. It makes me a little sad.

She looks at me again. "Burgundy, huh?"

"Great minds." I shrug, sheepishly. She turns back around before I can see what her expression is. Is she still mad about what happened? I mean, I can't blame her. But I'm wondering if it really is too late to make things right. I guess all I really can do is try.

Whatever conversation my parents were having with Justin faded away after Dillie walked in.

"Mom, Dad, Justin, y'all know Delia," I say, realizing how awkward that introduction was. "Delia, this is Mom, Dad . . . and Justin."

Dillie laughs it off and walks around the room, hugging Justin, shaking my dad's hand, and when she walks to my mom, my mom puts her hands on her shoulders and holds her at arm's length, drinking in her outfit.

"*So* beautiful. *Love* the burgundy," she says. She whispers something in Dillie's ear and Dillie howls, and they collapse with laughter into a hug. My dad and I raise our eyebrows at each other. I wonder what she said?

We have a few more minutes of polite banter before I check my watch again. It's 8:30. The performance is supposed to be at 9:00 p.m.

"Well, we'd best be heading out to our reservation," Dad says, taking my mom's hand and walking to the front door. "I hope there's no traffic. Y'all kids have a good time. Oh, and Darren?"

"Yes?" I say.

"Good lu—" he starts, but then my mom elbows him. "Never mind. We'll see y'all later!"

I scoff. "Have fun, y'all."

Mom winks at me before the door closes behind her. I asked them not to mention to Dillie or me about our relationship, the song, or the performance, because Dad would surely give it away.

"We should be heading out right behind them," I say as casually as I can. "Are y'all ready?"

"Sure!" Justin, Tiffany, and Dillie stand up.

"Um, my car doesn't have any more room, so Dillie, I was wondering if you'd be okay to ride with Darren?"

This is a terrible lie, with Justin driving a super-roomy car, but I don't say anything. I just look at Dillie.

"Well, I drove," she says.

I groan inwardly.

"But . . . I guess I could save my own gas." She smirks, walking slowly ahead of me, the back of her dress in full view. She looks beautiful from all angles.

We all walk outside. Justin and Tiffany get in his car, Dillie and I get in mine. I start the engine, and "Dillie's Song" blares from the speakers, the all-too-familiar lyrics and sound of my voice making me even more nervous.

"All right, all right, that was 'Dillie's Song.'" DJ Scoop's familiar voice talks over the song fading in the background. "I'll be DJing live at Jamison High School tonight, where the mysterious singer of 'Dillie's Song' will perform for the *first time at nine p.m.*! We'll finally get to see who it is. Stay tuned!"

"I don't know if you and Justin are trying to set me up to go to the dance with you," Dillie says. "But you do know that once the mystery singer meets me and sings . . . I will likely be hanging out with him." There is a ghost of a smile on her face. I can't tell if she is excited to hang out with this mystery singer, or if she is enjoying seeing me squirm.

"Of course," I say. "No worries." I see the time on the dashboard. It's 8:40 p.m.

Twenty minutes.

I tap the steering wheel at the red light. I've gotten to school from here in less than ten minutes. All I have to do is make sure I'm there to talk to the DJ before Miles gets onstage. . . .

"Oh, shoot!" Dillie exclaims. She groans and leans her head back against the seat.

"What's wrong?" I catch her eye. We catch another stoplight. We should be at the school in a little over five minutes. It'll be fine.

"I forgot my lipstick!"

"Your—huh?"

"My lipstick." She points to her lips. "I ordered this specifically because of how well it matches the dress! I can't *believe* I left it."

She rummages through her small purse again, eventually pouring the contents out onto her lap: a tiny bottle of perfume, a card holder, a twenty-dollar bill, her phone, tissue, and earring backs.

"You good?" I ask. I look at her lips. The color looks perfect.

"Yeah." She sighs. "I'll just have to be extra careful when I eat and drink." Her burgundy lips fix into a pout and she looks out of the passenger-side window.

I glance at the clock on the dashboard. It's 8:45 p.m. My stomach twists in knots, from nerves and everything else.

If Dillie's going to be thinking about her lipstick . . . she's not going to be in her best mood. One thing I learned from the podcast is that Dillie *loves* lipstick.

"How far is your house from here?" I say.

She looks over, her eyes wide. "It's only five minutes in the other direction," she replies. "Are you—going to take me to my house to get my lipstick?"

We will definitely miss my chance to perform if I do this. But I know the nagging feeling of leaving something at home. I lost my do-rag once and didn't feel right for the entire day until I got a new one.

I just need a new plan.

"Yeah. Let's go. Just tell me how to get there."

She points me in the direction of her house, and we're there in no time. I pull into the driveway of a duplex. The driveway is empty.

"My mom is on a date tonight, too," she says. "I guess all the adults took our homecoming dance as a way to get their alone time."

I'm wondering if she's going to just dash in and out, and whether I should keep the car running, when she asks, "Do you want to come inside? It'll only be a second."

I check the time on the dashboard before I turn the car off. Ten more minutes. But I can't tell her no. I don't even want to.

"Sure," I say. We walk to the door and my phone buzzes. Justin.

Justin: Where are you? It's almost 9!!
Darren: Dillie left something at her house. We're almost there.
Justin: Ok. We'll try to stall.
Darren: Thanks, bro.

"Tara, open the door!" Dillie yells, as she bangs on it. The door swings open. Tara has her hair in two buns, and her arms crossed.

"Back already?" She looks at me and smiles. "Hey, Darren!"

"Move," says Dillie, shoving her and going inside. "I need to get my lipstick."

She runs across the foyer and around the corner. "Darren, you can have a seat!" Her voice carries back to us.

I catch the clock on the wall. 8:52 p.m.

"You coming in, right?" her little sister says.

"Uh . . . yeah."

I step onto the welcome mat, close the door behind me, and walk into their home. It's a three-bedroom apartment, with Dillie's apparently being on the left, along with another room, probably her sister's. The other bedroom, probably her mom's, was on the right. I sit on the couch and rub my hands on my slacks. Tara disappears into the kitchen.

> *Stop whatever you're doing*
> *Stop whatever you're doing*

My heart thumps. I hear the song again, playing in the distance somewhere. For a split second I think it's coming from the school, but I realize Tara's watching someone's eClips and they are using my song in the background.

I wonder if Justin is still able to stall. I check my phone again and see no updates from him. That's good.

But then I realize I have to sing. In front of everyone. In just a few minutes.

Again, the thought of just not doing it creeps into my head. I mean, it's not like I *have* to.

Okay. Relax, I tell myself. *You know this song like the back of your hand. It's* your *song. You've been practicing.*

I hum to get control of my nerves.

And Dillie D, you're my favorite girl

"Hey."

I look up, realizing that I'm humming. I stop. Tara is staring at me and pointing.

"Hey." She stands up and walks toward me. "Are you the—?"

I start waving my hands and head back and forth in such a fast motion, it catches Tara off guard, and she scoffs and steps back.

Good.

"Don't say anything. Please! I want it to be a surprise for Dillie," I hiss. I don't have time to try to convince her it's not me.

Her sneer suddenly turns into a wide smile, exactly like her sister's. "Aww! That's—"

"Tara, have you seen my lipstick?" Dillie comes into the living room, her eyes narrowed.

"O—Oh. The burgundy one?"

Dillie says nothing, but glares at her sister. Tara runs into her room. My phone buzzes again.

Justin: Bro, where are you?! Don't tell me you chickened out!

We need to leave right now.

Tara is still in her room.

Dillie sucks her teeth. "Hurry up!" she yells.

Come on, Tara, I think.

After what seems like hours, Tara comes back into the living room holding a small tube and wearing a bashful grin.

"I just wanted to see how it would look on me. I wish I was going to the dance." Tara pouts, the same way Dillie did in the car, and Dillie snatches the lipstick out of her hand.

"We gotta go. We're already running later than I wanted to."

"I've finished all my chores, too, you know."

"Good. See you later."

"Can I come? *Please?* All I have to do is put on my dress. You know I'm not allowed to wear makeup yet, so that's all I'd have to do."

Dillie turns back around and looks at her sister.

We do not have time for this, I think to myself. If Tara knows I'm the singer, why won't she let us leave on time for the performance?

Then I realize. She wants to go to the school because she knows I'm the singer and she wants to see the performance. That's a nice thought—Tara watching her sister getting serenaded by the mystery singer.

"Tara, you know I would let you come but you're grounded and I'm probably staying out late tonight," Dillie says. "If Mama comes back and sees I took you, *I'd* be grounded, too, and I can't have that."

"I can come back with my friend Suzie. Her curfew is at eleven. Her parents are picking her up."

"Tara, don't you know if her parents are bringing you back, they're going to bring it up to Mama next time they see her? Then you'll be caught. I gotta teach you some things, little sis."

But not right now, I think. But I can't think it—I *have* to say something.

"The mystery singer will be performing any minute," I say to Dillie. "Justin just texted me and said he's about to get onstage. People will be looking for you."

"But I thought—"

Dillie whips back around to look at her sister. I take this chance to throw my hands in the air in a silent "Exactly, it's me! That's why I have to get to the school ASAP!" motion to Tara.

Tara's eyes get wide over her sister's shoulder, and she says, "Never mind. I don't want to go anymore."

Dillie looks surprised. "Really? Why?"

"I just—I mean. My grounding ends tomorrow anyway. I'd rather just wait it out."

Dillie smiles at her sister. "Now you're starting to get it, T! You know what, I'm proud of you."

Dillie starts to walk over to her sister, her arms out for a hug, but Tara yells, "No! Leave! Go to the dance! Hurry! Oh and uh—tell the mystery singer that I'll be needing an autograph." Then she turns and runs into her room and shuts the door.

Dillie stares at the closed door for a second, then turns to me. "Well, that's Tara for you. Are you ready?"

I nod, and we make our way outside. My phone is buzzing nonstop, but I can't check it yet.

Finally, we get to the school. I help Dillie out of the car since she stated the parking lot was not kind to the long, skinny heel on her shoes, and we follow the heavy bassline to the gym. All I have to do is get inside and tell Dillie I need to use the restroom and everything else will fall into place.

We reach the gym and I breathe a little to check my phone and see where Justin is.

I take out my phone.

Two missed calls and a text from Justin.

Justin: WHERE ARE YOU

The lights in the gym are dim. On the opposite side of the big, crowded space, there is a stage set up, with a DJ booth beside it.

Suddenly, I am hit with a swarm of nerves. I can't do this, I can't.

"Well, I am going to go to the front, so I can get a good view of the mystery singer," Dillie says to me. "Thanks for the ride, and thank you for taking me to get my lipstick. I—I hope you have a good time," she says. She looks at me deeply, as if she wants to say something, or that she's waiting on *me* to say something. I look back into her eyes. In this moment, I want to tell her the truth, but she will find out in just a little while. Plus, I'm so nervous I can't say anything back. After a few seconds of silence, she walks away.

I could just leave. I'm still right beside the door. I could slip out, right now. Tell Justin and Tiffany that I was having technical difficulties. Justin will never let me hear the end of it, but who cares.

I step back outside to get some air. I lean against the brick of the gym and breathe the cool autumn air in deeply. I try to imagine different versions of this night, some good, some bad.

The worlds I create for myself are so vivid: one where I am singing and I am booed off the stage. I can hear the crowd, feel the disappointment. One where I am singing and the crowd loves it. I can hear the cheers, feel the excitement, the accomplishment. One where I am singing but Dillie is still mad afterward, or uninterested. I can feel the mixture of disappointment and peace, hear the echo of my own song in my head. One where I am singing and it all goes well. My heart swells.

I open my eyes and my eyes fill with the school parking lot, all those emotions washing away. Whatever version happens tonight, I want to feel it for real. I want the memory, not just the thought.

I walk past the entrance, to the side door, so I'm not seen.

"The man behind the hottest song in the streets right now!" I hear DJ Scoop say. "Y'all have been wondering who is this person, this new R&B singer on the scene, and you're about to find out right *now.*"

26: Breakout Star

I open my eyes.

I'm onstage.

Everyone is looking at me. Some are laughing, with their phones already out and pointed at me. Anticipating a joke.

I don't care. People may talk over or try to speak for me, but one thing nobody will do is outsing me.

Not tonight.

I hear the familiar chords of the song.

I clear my throat, say a small prayer, and take a deep breath. Finally, I open my mouth, thankful for the vocal warm-ups I decided to do a few short minutes ago.

> *Stop whatever you're doing*
> *Stop whatever you're doing*

"Darren?" I hear someone's voice. Dillie's. I catch her eye in the crowd, her eyebrows knitted together in confusion. Shock. The mumbles in the crowd get louder.

The first note, I hear people gasp. I can't hear myself, because the crowd is getting louder and louder, saying things like, "Wait, that's *him?*"

"Listen!"

"He's in my math class!"

More phones are out, and I'm looking straight ahead, I can't even look at Dillie until—

Stop whatever you're doing
Stop whatever you're doing
Dillie D in the Place to Be *is on*
And you better be tuned in

Sundays at 3:00 p.m. keep it locked
Dillie D in your speaker box,
No better podcast in the world
And Delia D, you're my favorite girl

I make a show of saying Delia instead of Dillie, changing the key, so she can really know that *she's* my favorite girl, not just the version of her on her podcast.

Her friends Mia and Julie grab her arms and scream things at her, at each other, as she stands there, her eyes glittering, her mouth, covered in her beloved burgundy lipstick, opening in surprise.

Dillie D in the Place to Be, *you are the girl I'm pursuing*
In love with the fragrance you're using
No time for fakes I'm assuming

I continue, and the crowd gets loud again, this time laughing.

Did I hit the wrong note? I think, singing anyway. I see a flicker of movement beside me.

I'm almost to my favorite part of the song. This is happening. The bass is vibrating through my chest, the same way it does in the car. The lights above my head are hot; the stage shakes with every step I take. I hear my voice, and I'm not nervous. The crowd is blurred, except for the beautiful girl in burgundy, front and center. I want to take in every minute.

But I want to make this dream a reality
Together just you and me, we
Complement each other so nicely

The DJ turns the song up again, so I hear my voice amplified over . . . my voice. I layer over the recording, with new harmonies, more vibrato, singing the way I want to in this moment.

"Oh my gosh! Go, Darren! You better sing!" I hear Tiffany say.

I force myself to look at Dillie. So I can remember her face tonight when I replay this moment in my head, over and over again.

She's watching me, her grin faded into a small smirk playing at the corner of her lips. It feels like there is a spotlight on her.

With a big note, I finish the song, and the crowd breaks out into applause.

"Well, it looks like the secret is officially out!" the DJ says, at his booth. Justin, Tiffany, Jerrod, and—is that *Zoe?*—are standing beside the DJ booth.

"The mystery singer has proven to be none other than Darren Armstrong. Congrats, Darren! I hope you're ready because your life is about to change."

I feel my phone in my pocket vibrating nonstop. I wonder if people are texting me, tagging me in videos.

I catch Justin's eye and nod. He whispers something to DJ Scoop, and hands him something. I stand onstage awkwardly.

"Okay, it looks like Darren has prepared something else for y'all," DJ says. "I have the track right here in my hand. It's called 'Rhythm and Muse.'"

The beginning of another one of Jerrod's tracks starts, and I nod my head to it. The crowd doesn't know this one, so only a few people sway to the beat. People still have their phones out.

My nerves are building up, but I'm working hard to channel them into excitement. So many thoughts are competing for the front row in my mind—how I look, how I sound, what people will think, but I let them build up, without acknowledging them right now. I will release them through my song. For this moment to be right, I need to be in the moment, putting my all into it.

"This is my newest song. It came straight from the heart," I say, as I'm waiting for the beat to the drop. "I hope y'all enjoy it. Here we go."

Here we go.

I take a deep breath and walk closer to the edge of the stage, closer to Dillie and sing, forcing myself not to lose eye contact.

She's smiling, but it's a different one. One I've never seen before.

[CHORUS]
I can be your rhythm
You can be my muse
I can be your boyfriend, baby
If that's what you choose
You can be my inspiration
It's not infatuation
It's real
So let me tell you how I feel

[VERSE 1]
My thoughts are a steady rhythm of you
A repetition of your smile, girl, it's true
I hear your name on every beat
And it makes me wanna sing
Make a melody of just us two

[PRE-CHORUS]
I told you I'm often mistaken for a shy guy

> *But now I'm putting myself out there,*
> *on the line*

I sing the chorus again, and the words float out of my mouth, into the microphone, through the speakers.

> *[VERSE 2]*
> *I knew we would*
> *Make the perfect duet*
> *But I also knew*
> *That I had to come correct*
> *I knew that time was of the essence*
> *But when I'm in your presence*
> *My thoughts are like*
> *A song on repeat*
> *I felt like I couldn't speak*
> *So I needed to sing*
> *To show you what I mean, oh*
>
> *I'm often mistaken for a shy guy*
> *But I just like to take my time*

I sing the chorus one more time before I prepare myself for the bridge, where I challenge myself vocally. I can't help myself. Before I do, I peek another look at Dillie and she smiles. I smile back, and I hear some people in the crowd go "Aww."

Since I'm not in my comfort zone anyway, I decide to do something completely out of the ordinary. I walk down the stairs and stop right in front of Dillie. I grab her hands and stare straight into her eyes. The warmth of her hands takes the nerves away.

[BRIDGE]
Like nineties Rhythm and Blues
We can be just as classic
As twenties Rhythm and Muse
We'll be far from average
We'd share that same
Feeling of love
Feeling of grooves
Me and you
Together we can't lose.

I sing the chorus one more time as the track fades out. The applause around me is so loud, but I'm not focusing on that. I don't even register what the DJ is saying.

I picture my original Delia Daydream, where a crowd is chanting our name in unison. But this time, it's real.

"Darren!"

"Delia!"

"Darren!"

"Delia!"

I'm just looking at Dillie, still holding her hand, when she lets go and looks at me.

Oh no. Did I do something wrong?

"It was you, all this time!" she says, laughing. Before I realize what's happening, she wraps her arms around me and plants a big kiss on my lips. I squeeze her tight and kiss her back, the cheers around us getting louder.

This was definitely better than anything I could've imagined.

27: Harmony

The next morning, Dillie, Justin, Tiffany, Jerrod, Destiny, and I are piled into a booth at Sally's, stuffed from the burgers and fries and ice cream and everything else we ordered for the table.

Justin looks at yet another eClip of last night, featuring my song "Rhythm and Muse." "Whoa! Darren, did you know that your song was the Clip Feature of the night last night? It was one of the most used songs on all of eClips!"

I shrug. I knew that, and I also knew that the real version of "Dillie's Song" was right up there with it. Of course it's cool, but now I'm realizing opinions are like waves. They're high and low, they come and go. As long as I'm happy with the songs, that's all that matters to me.

"What's the next move, y'all?" Destiny asks, her bottom grill, identical to Jerrod's, catching the light. She and Dillie became friends at the dance last night and exchanged numbers.

Dillie yawns. "The next move is my bed. I'm tired."

"Same here," I say. After the dance was over, Justin spent the night at my house and we went to church this morning—the *early* service. But I wanted to have enough time to talk to the youth choir director about potentially joining again.

"Yeah, my dad wants me to help him cut grass after we leave here." Justin groans and puts his head down on the table. "I'm mad just thinking about it."

"I don't feel like doing anything else today," I say. The homecoming dance was one of the best nights of my life, something I'll always remember when I think about high school. I'd rather lie in bed and replay the night, fall into my Sunday nap until Dillie's show comes on and it's time for dinner. And when I wake up, Dillie will be coming over to try Dad's lasagna.

"Don't worry, baby, my homeboy is having an after-party for the car show that's happening downtown. *We* can go to that," Jerrod says, grabbing her hand, and Destiny kisses his cheek.

Yeah. I definitely don't want to go to that.

"How did you two even get inside the dance last night?" I ask him, as I finish the rest of my ice cream.

"What do you mean?" Jerrod asks, his mouth full.

"You don't even go to our school, man. I thought it was for Jamison students only."

"Yeah, I know." He swallows his food but says nothing else.

"Jerrod was technically my plus-one since Tiffany didn't need one," Justin says, reaching for a few of his fries. "Destiny . . . hmm, I don't know how Destiny got there."

"Well?" Dillie asks.

We look toward Jerrod and Destiny, and they stare back

mischievously, daring us to ask again. Forget it, maybe I don't want to know.

Jerrod changes the subject. "Aye, y'all remember the DJ last night? He asked who produced the song and I told him I did. He gave me his information and told me he'd put me in contact with some local rappers who were looking for some new tracks." He grins, his own bottom grill catching the light.

"Oh, man, that's dope!" Justin says. "Hey, your beats are really good. I've told you that before. You could charge a pretty penny for them."

"Yeah, but I'm not selling any until we figure out which ones Darren wants for his EP."

At that, everyone looks at me.

"EP? When will it release?" Dillie asks.

"What's the name of it?" Tiffany asks.

"I want to hear it first," Justin says.

"Definitely not. You might leak it," I accuse, and we laugh. "You'll see," I say in response to the rest of the questions. "I may share a little bit more on *Dillie D.* Next week."

"So Dillie, I gotta know," Justin starts. "Did you think that Darren could be the mystery singer?"

Everyone at the table looks at Dillie, including me. She's wearing a smirk that turns into a big smile. She takes a big, dramatic breath.

As if on cue, my phone rings and it's a call from my mom.

I look back at Dillie, trying to get the answer out of her before I answer the phone. She gestures for me to answer it, so I do.

I answer it.

"Hey, Mom," I say. Dillie squeezes closer to me and waves.

"Oh, baby, you did such an amazing job! Zoe just showed us the video from last night." My mom's voice and face come through the phone my sister is holding, her arm outstretched toward me. Zoe comes in the frame briefly. "Congrats, knucklehead. You did so good. We left right after, when the DJ started playing music and everyone started jumping around to that new rapper. I'm *too* old for that."

I scoff. "Thanks, sis." Leave it to Zoe to become a freshman in college and act like a senior citizen.

The phone shifts again. "Congrats, son! I knew you had it in you!" Dad shuffles a bit to get more in the frame, but now I can't see Mom anymore.

"Dad, you know we could've just done a group video chat, right?" I hear Zoe's voice laughing at our parents. "So that we could all see each other at the same time?"

"Oh, we don't have to do all of that," my mom says. "Put the camera on Delia." I oblige, holding the phone toward her.

"So, what did you think? Oh, it was so hard to keep the secret, Darren's father almost blurted it out, I know it—"

"No I wasn't!" Dad's face comes back on the screen. "I wasn't going to say anything!"

"Dad, Mom," I say, hearing Dillie's laugh in my ear above it all. "Can we talk about this when I get back to the house? We're almost finished eating." I know they are only two sentences away from embarrassing me.

"Oh! See, Wyatt? We're disturbing them! It was his idea to call, you know! Love you, see you later!"

After talking to Sally a little bit, we all hug and part ways in the parking lot.

"Are we still on for tomorrow?" I ask. I reach over, my hand searching for Dillie's. She grabs it and it sends warmth through my body. We're recording the newest episode of *Dillie D* after school.

"Yup." She nods, her eyes sparkling in the sun. "I can't wait."

We kiss and I walk her to her car. She sits in the driver's seat and cranks it up, and I hear a voice—my voice—taking over the radio.

"This is the newest from Darren Armstrong, the not-so-mysterious mystery man behind the hit 'Dillie's Song,'" DJ Scoop says. "Last night was something straight out of a romantic comedy, but we'll talk about that more later. Here's his newest track, which he premiered last night, called 'Rhythm and Muse.'"

Dillie squeals. "Darren! Listen! It's you!"

I smile. "So, do you like this one?"

She looks at me. "Do I like it? No."

I swallow. *It's okay*, I think. *As long as I like it, that's all that—*

"I *love* it!"

She closes her eyes and sings the words, off-key, and it's music to my ears.

I listen to the song on my way home and think about what it could mean for me. I don't know if I want to be famous, or if this song will even *make* me famous, but we'll cross that bridge when we come to it. I'm just happy to be doing what I love again.

I pull into my driveway and cut my own voice off, taking in the quiet. I listen to the cicadas and a bass booming somewhere in the distance, feeling the chilly fall air around me.

I say a prayer, just two words. "Thank you."

I turn the key to my peaceful house, walk upstairs, past Zoe's room. The familiar sound of her loud snoring permeates the hallway. My parents are in the kitchen, and I say a quick hello to them before I announce that I'm taking a nap.

I sit on the bed and look at the yellow legal pad I got from Incredible Beatz. Jack told me I could keep it for good. It's a good thing too, because it's ripped, scribbled on, and even water damaged in some places. I flip to the first page, where I wrote the first draft of "Dillie's Song." A few pages later, to "Rhythm and Muse." I notice something written on some random page in the middle, and I flip to it.

There's curly purple handwriting.

I knew
I knew
I knew
It was always you.
XO Dillie.

I drop the notepad and pick it back up to reread that sentence what feels like five hundred times.

Dillie knew?

When . . . ?

How . . . ?

I call her.

"Hello?" she answers the phone. She's lying in bed, wearing a huge purple bonnet that almost takes over the screen.

"Dillie," I ask her. "You knew?"

She laughs. I glance at my own face on-screen and at how shocked I look, and try to shift my expression into something more neutral, but I can't. "So you found my note, huh?"

"Yes! *How?*"

"Duh, Darren!" She props herself up on her elbow. "How could I not?"

Was I really that obvious, all this time?

"Well, you have to understand how many times I've listened to 'Dillie's Song,'" she continues. "I knew the person who wrote those words had to love music. And be, I don't know, kind of romantic. I always thought it was pretty obvious the more we started hanging out that Darren the mystery singer and Darren

Armstrong were the same person. It's kind of hard to separate the two, right? But then, I had my doubts once you didn't ask me to the dance and the 'mystery singer' did."

I wait for myself to feel ridiculous or embarrassed, but the feeling doesn't come. It *is* hard to separate the two. It was always just . . . me.

"Yeah . . . I guess it is. Kind of like Dillie D and Delia Dawson?"

"*Kind* of. Although, I could be more true to myself. I'm going to take a few weeks off and use our interview as the season finale. You know, and try that 'break from your passion' thing you're always talking about. I'm going to restructure my podcast and have a mentorship episode once a month, and an interview episode once a month. A little variety, you know?"

"I'm proud of you," I tell her. I really am. I know that wasn't easy to do. "Well, at least you'll have one listener. Me." I chuckle.

A small snort comes through the phone. "Thank *you*. You know, you did surprise me. Which is saying something because I'm not very easy to surprise. I'm just too nosy."

"I guess this Cinder-fella fit the profile after all," I say.

"Oh my gosh, one of my corniest jokes ever." She groans.

"Just wait until I get us matching Queen Charming and Cinder-fella shirts."

"You wouldn't."

"Yeah, I probably wouldn't."

I notice I'm walking around in circles in my room and I stop at my window. I lean against it and close my eyes.

"Sleepy?" Dillie asks.

I open my eyes and see her face. I smile.

"No, just ready to relax. So, when did you write that note in my legal pad?"

"Who knows? Did I write it during the lock-in? Or when all of those papers fell out of the visor in your car? Or at Sally's . . . ?"

"So, you're really not going to tell me, huh?"

"Not *just* yet."

I smile at her. It's cool. Another thing to daydream about.

I tell her I'll call her later. The past few days have been a whirlwind and I want to take advantage of the peace. To hear my thoughts. To be content.

My phone is buzzing with so many calls, texts, messages, and tags. I turn the sound off. I change into my favorite Spider-Man shirt and pajama pants, lie on the bed, and stare straight at the ceiling. The house is completely silent. I don't even hear my sister's snoring. Something crinkles under me and I realize it's the sheet music for the song I'm using to audition for section leader next week. Something classical and different for me.

With my audition for section leader and youth choir coming up, not to mention my studio sessions for my EP, my appearance on Dillie's show, and emails I've been getting to perform at local festivals and school dances, I have a *lot* of thinking to do and a lot of decisions to make. Right now, though, I just want to replay last night, over and over and over again in my head. Is it another Delia Daydream? Sure. This time, though, I can still feel Dillie's lips against mine, smell her perfume, see her dress, and hear the music. This time, I can hear my voice echo through the gym, see the looks of my friends, and feel that feeling of doing something I love to do.

This time, it's real.

28: Outro

DILLIE D IN THE PLACE TO BE, EPISODE 51 NOTES: MYSTERY SINGER REVEALED

> *Stop whatever you're doing*
> *Stop whatever you're doing*
> Dillie D in the Place to Be *is on*
> *And you better be tuned in*
> *Sundays at 3:00 p.m. keep it locked*
> *Dillie D in your speaker box,*
> *No better podcast in the world*
> *And Dillie D, you're my favorite girl*

Dillie: And by now we *all* know who is singing that song, our guest for today's show, tweaked just the tiniest bit to fit the vibe of my show. Everyone, welcome Darren Armstrong, the not-so-mysterious mystery singer, and . . . I mean, I guess I'll tell them—my new boyfriend.

[Applause track]

Dillie: Welcome to the season finale of *Dillie D and the Place to Be*. Darren, I'm so happy to have you on the show today.

Darren: I'm happy to be here.

Dillie: Did you ever think you'd be here, like this? On my show?

Darren: [pauses]: Yes and no. I've thought about us being together, but I've never really pictured being on the show. I like it, though.

Dillie: We have a bunch of questions today, including how and why this whole mystery singer thing started. Let's work backward. We hear you're coming out with an EP soon, on the heels of the hit single, also known as my theme song, "Dillie's Song." The next one, "Rhythm and Muse," is already getting major streams after less than a week. How do you feel?

Darren: It's a lot to take in, honestly, I'm *still* taking it in. But I'm happy and excited for what's to come. The EP is just in the beginning stages, but I already have a few songs written for it.

Dillie: This is all happening in the midst of junior year, too. We're not far off from SATs, prom, college applications. Is this something you want to take big? Like, do you want to be a famous singer? Or a super low-key artist who just drops projects when he feels like it? Have you thought about how you're going to juggle everything?

Darren: I've thought about all of this, and I have ideas about how it's all going to play out. Right now, I'm just focused on school— gotta say school because my mom is listening, hey, Ma—applying for college, making new music for my EP . . . enjoying my new relationship and hanging out with my friends. My plan right now is to focus on those things and make music that makes me happy. As far as making it big . . . I want to sing. Maybe even for a living. A famous singer? I'm not sure about all that yet. I'm figuring things out as I go.

Dillie: I'm glad to hear that. You've heard me say it on the show and in person before, but you have an amazing voice.

Darren: *laughs* Thank you. I think so, too.

Acknowledgments

I got the idea to write this novel in 2018. During that time, I wasn't seeing a lot of romance centered around a teenage, Black, male protagonist, and I felt like they deserved to have their happily ever after, too. Since writing this, I've given birth to two sons, and I'm excited that they can see themselves on these pages.

As always, I thank God and Jesus for giving me this passion to write. I am so grateful to be able to do what I love for a living.

My husband, Rob: Thank you for answering my millions of music questions, talking through scenes and scenarios with me, taking me to studio sessions for research, and just being you.

Bear and August: My babies! Bear made his debut while I was writing this novel, and August made his debut during editing. I can't wait for you both to read this one day.

Holly, I am always so grateful to be a part of Team Root! Thank you for always championing for me.

Jen and the Quill Tree Books and HarperCollins family: I can't thank you enough for giving this book of mine a chance. With every ramble, concern, or idea of mine, I have always felt that you were in my corner, and I am so grateful for that!

My brother Eli: In the early drafts, Darren was a lot like you, but both you and Darren have grown throughout the years of me writing this! Thank you for being you.

The Browns, the Hills, and the Holidays: Thank you for everything!

Deshawn, my cousin, my inspiration for Jerrod—except you can actually RAP!

Mommy, thank you for always giving me the freedom to explore my creativity and love for reading, be myself, and quit jobs I hated. It paid off!!

Tony, Deshawn, Marcel, Harrison, Erik, Jalyle, and Alex: Young Black boys and men in my family and life who I am always rooting for!

To the readers: Thank you for taking the time to pick up my novel. I truly hope it made you smile.